DOWN THE LINE

More Surfing Stories

By

John McLean

Copyright © John McLean 2003

Published by Winter Productions
21 Wigmore Street, London W1U 1PJ

ISBN 1-872970-27-3

Cover Design and photography: Daniel Harrison

Printed through Colorcraft Ltd., Hong Kong for Winter Productions 21 Wigmore Street, London W1U 1PJ, Great Britain.

To my Geordie mates

Sam, Andrew, Joel, Davey, Trev, Jed, Richard and Gabe

ABOUT THE AUTHOR

John McLean, one of the best known surf writers in Europe, has written many articles for British and French surf magazines over the years. He is also the author of *Island of the Gods*, a surfing novel set on the island of Bali. In 1998 he wrote his first book of surfing short stories, *Deep Inside*; his other novels are *Traffic Jam* and *Tartan Dragon*

Other books of surfing fiction by the same author

Island of the Gods 578 pages   Price: £6

Adrian goes to Bali on a surfing holiday and falls in love with the beautiful Dayu. The story is packed with interesting characters, wild parties, strange Balinese customs and wonderful sessions in the waves at Kuta Reef, Padang Padang and Uluwatu.

Deep Inside 198 pages   Price £5

A collection of eighteen short stories that cover many aspects of surfing - the camaraderie of the line-up, surf trips to exotic spots, beach life, localism, after surf activities and other adventures. Funny, reflective, irreverent and stimulating.

These books are available at the above prices (which include postage) from the author, John McLean, 21 Wigmore St., London W1U 1PJ, United Kingdom. Add £1 per book for postage to countries other than Britain.

CHAPTERS

CHAPTER ONE

A SIGN OF DISTRESS

What made surfing at Pineapple Point so special was that the deep green of the sub-tropical foliage came right down to the sandy beach; from out in the line-up the shore appeared as natural and unspoilt as when Captain Cook first sailed up this part of the Queensland coast in 1770.

Most of the area was a national park although there were one or two pockets of private land that were left over from the time before the park was created. On one of these plots stood the Ocean Wave, a small cafe/bar with a big wooden deck that overlooked the point. It was at the end of an unpaved road; after an energy sapping session in the waves it was only a few steps through the banana and mango trees up to the Ocean Wave to get rid of the after-surf munchies.

From the tables outside on the deck surfers in sunbleached baggies watched the others in the waves while eating their salad rolls and listening to the strains of Dire Straits which thumped out of the stereo. Dripping rash vests hung over the wooden railings while their owners sat for hours at the tables playing cards and backgammon, watching surf videos and enjoying endless smokes while waiting for the surf to pick up. When that happened and the waves got really big, the spray would sometimes shower the deck, adding an extra pinch or two of salt to the rolls and burgers.

The cafe was run by a young married couple who were known to everyone as Dick and Bella. "Dick the Trick" was also a surfer and, when the cafe was not too busy, he would put on his boardies and rash vest and join his customers out in the waves. Dick and his cafe were as much a part of the surf scene as Pineapple Point and the waves themselves.

All went well until the wretched council decided to pave the road that led through the trees to the cafe. This was simply the latest step in their campaign to draw to the area well-heeled tourists who would spend money in the shops and hotels which, of course, were owned by the councillors themselves.

The upgrading of a road is always a sign of danger and Pineapple Point was no exception. Instead of only surfers trudging along the broken, unpaved road to the Ocean Wave big, expensive cars were now to be seen swooping into the area and disgorging over-dressed tourists with cameras who took photos of trees, dropped litter everywhere and even threw still burning cigarette butts on to the tinder dry ground.

However, the catalyst occurred one afternoon when all the boys were out in the waves and Dick and his wife had turned down the music while they got on with their work of cleaning the tables and preparing more burgers for when the crew would paddle back in and head for their feeding ground. The only sounds were the laughing of the kookaburras in the trees and the intermittent breaking of the waves.

When Dick looked up and saw the customer he was a little surprised; not the usual dripping hair and boardies but red sports trousers with knife edge creases, a royal blue shirt and cravat and polished white shoes. Short, oily black hair starting to go grey and a mobile phone hanging from his belt. Dick thought that he looked like the Australian flag upside down.

The man and his wife, who seemed to have a permanent scowl on her face, ordered two coffees and some raisin toast and went outside to sit at a table on the deck. Dick could hear them discussing the beauty of the setting and declaiming in loud voices how many thousands of dollars such a place would be worth if it was on the edge of Melbourne.

Dick had been working like a Trojan for more than an hour and so, after serving the two customers, he poured himself a cold beer and sat down at a table on the deck for a few minutes' relaxation.

"How long have you had this place?" asked the man as he turned his chair around to face the proprietor.

"Six years. Six years of very hard work. Seven days a week. Starting with breakfast at half past seven."

"Your prices are very cheap."

"Most of our customers are surfers. They're not all that rich. It's really a surfers' bar."

"Now that's where you are wrong. I'm a real estate developer and I know what a place like this would be worth if it was an up-market restaurant. If you could get a well-heeled clientele you would be able to serve meals for five or six times the prices that are on your board. And for much less work too. Just lunches and dinners. That way you and your wife wouldn't have to get up so early in the mornings. You could buy a bottle of wine for five dollars and sell it to your diners for twenty - no trouble at all. And people usually buy four or five bottles and then finish up with a liqueur. With all the credit cards these days it is just spend, spend, spend."

"But how could I be certain that people would turn up?" asked Dick hesitantly. "At the moment I've got a sure clientele with all the surfers. Better the devil you know and all that."

"Listen, I'm from Melbourne and I know that people would spend big bucks to dine at such an exotic place as this. It's unique. Look at the way this banana leaf is growing over the deck and touching my shoulder as I eat. This is something that people can't do in Sydney and Melbourne; when they come up here for a sub-tropical holiday, it's just the type of thing they want."

He pulled out a notebook and started writing down sets of figures - numbers of diners multiplied by the expected cost of a meal, rough costs and profit margins. He showed them to Dick whose interest was starting to be aroused.

"People like us are the silvertails," declared the upside down Australian flag. "We don't mind paying top rates for a first class meal in attractive surroundings. And the more exotic the location, the more you can charge. People would be happy to pay big prices for fresh fish caught in the bay. You should listen to those of us who know the value of these things."

A couple of surfers walked up the wooden steps on to the deck. They leaned their boards against the front wall of the cafe and hung their rash vests over the wooden railing. One of them walked over to the stereo and turned it on. Then they sat down at a table and ordered double pineapple burgers and chips.

"Just one thing," said the man in a low voice as Dick got up to service their order. "You'd have to get rid of all these surfers. We silvertails would not want to come to a place where people walk around half naked with salt water dripping out of their hair and sand on their feet."

That night, as they were washing the last of the dishes, Dick discussed with his wife what the man had said. And the more they talked about it, the more attractive it seemed. Sleep-ins in the morning. Less customers for more money. "I think we deserve a bit of a break from the long hours," declared Bella, "and this could well be it. I know how to do French country cooking....."

The first sign of change came the following week when Dick put up a sign saying that the cafe would be closed for a week for renovations. Naturally his surfer customers were interested. After all, it was almost a second home to them where they spent a good part of each day. Some of them asked what kind of renovations but Dick was evasive.

"Oh well, we'll just have to wait until it's all finished and see what it looks like," they concluded. But when it reopened, they all got a rude shock.

The menu, which was displayed at the entrance to the deck, showed prices that, in the opinion of his regular customers, were somewhere in the stratosphere. And anyway, it was now three course lunches and dinners only. No more snacks. And what about the big sign next to the menu? "Gentlemen must wear a tie or cravat. Shoes must be worn at all times. No thongs allowed."

Dick decided to have a big opening night which was advertised in the local tourist information office and at the hotels where the silvertails stayed. Everything was prepared by midday so he decided to go for a quick surf and then come in and do the last minute tasks. But, even though he was in the line-up for more than an hour, he never got a wave; he was dropped in on every time. And he was no longer "Dick the Trick" but "Dick the Prick".

After they came in from surfing some of the regulars gathered on the beach. There was nowhere else for them to go as they had not brought their ties and polished shoes. There seemed to be two schools of thought: those who were ready to go and set a match to the place immediately and those who said that, since it was Dick's restaurant and he had to pay the bills, then surely he had the right to do what he liked with his own property. The course of action on which they eventually agreed lay somewhere between these two extremes.

Ronnie said that he knew "Snake Lady", a fairly busty woman of about thirty who, in the evenings, stripped down to a silver bikini and did a snake dance with a live python in a tourist restaurant in town. "I know that she sleeps with her favourite python but she might be prepared to sell us one of the others," he said. They discussed it further and then entrusted Ronnie with the task of making the approach.

When he arrived at Snake Lady's wooden bungalow he told her of their little problem and she was immediately sympathetic. She liked surfers - especially really young ones - almost as much as she liked snakes and expressed her willingness to help.

"Even if you have to part with a python?" he asked.

"Yes, so long as it's not Jeremiah; he's my favourite. We're known as a "couple" in the restaurant. You could have Sabrina; she's been a bit sick lately." She led him out to the kitchen where several pythons and boa constrictors were writhing around on the bench.

With darkness came the first of the silvertails in their big, shiny cars. They swanned up the steps and on to the romantically lit deck of the tarted up restaurant. Most of them were real estate agents and second hand car dealers but they all had shoes and ties and cravats and lots of credit cards in their pockets and that was all that mattered.

The restaurant reviewer of the local newspaper also turned up with a photographer as he had been persuaded by Dick to feature the big first night in the next issue.

And what a night it was! Lots of fresh fish, many bottles of wine that Dick sold at the price that the upside down Australian flag had suggested and a general atmosphere of laughter and merriment. The kitchen was a hive of frenzied activity as the bills for each table zoomed up into three figure amounts. Not all the activity, however, was on the deck; some of it was underneath.

Ronnie, with the python stuffed into a wire cage, approached the cafe from the back where he was well hidden by the dark leaves of the banana trees. It was easy for him to wriggle underneath the floorboards as, like most structures in that part of Queensland, the cafe rested on thick posts that rose three feet above the ground as a protective measure against termites and white ants. He waited until most of the happy and half drunk diners were on to their dessert before crawling under the deck and releasing Sabrina from the cage and through a small gap between two of the floorboards. Then he crawled back under the cafe and darted silently through the trees without waiting to witness the results of his action.

The first of the diners to become aware of the python was Kaye Smith who, after three bottles of Hunter Valley red, was playing footsies with her husband as they picked away at the last of their seafood platter of oysters, mussels, crayfish, king prawns and Moreton Bay bugs. "Stop it," she giggled, "Take your foot away. And why is it so slippery? It feels as if you've pulled your trouser leg up and rubbed some oil on it."

"What are you talking about/" he replied. "You've had too much to drink. Both my feet are safely under my chair."

"You can't fool me."

"Have a look if you don't believe me."

"I will."

She lifted the side of the tablecloth and peered underneath. Her sudden scream stopped all the other diners in mid conversation. Her husband jumped up from his chair and so did some of the others. In the dim candlelight could be detected a long, unwinding coil that was starting to glide across the dark wooden deck.

"My God, it's a python!" yelled a man who had been drinking continuously since six o'clock. "Like in the Garden of Eden. It must be Satan himself." The screaming women were now running towards the steps so as to get off the dangerous deck as quickly as possible. And the men were not far behind.

In the mad scramble Kaye Smith tripped on the top step and fell down to the bottom, fracturing her leg in the process. She lay there howling in agony with the others running over the top of her in their highly polished shoes with stiletto heels.

The only one to stay on the deck was the photographer from the local newspaper who could not believe his luck in actually being at the scene of an incident instead of having to rush along afterwards, which was usually the case. Snap! Snap! Snap! For a few moments Sabrina was the most photographed snake in the whole world.

No one knew what to do - not even Dick the Trick who was just as petrified as all the others. One of the silvertails had dined the previous night at the Chinese restaurant at the other end of the road and he had the presence of mind to grab his mobile phone and ring Mister Wong to tell him that his services were required immediately to capture a python at the Ocean Wave.

Mister Wong picked up a garden spade and drove fast along the road to the scene of action. He had a big smile on his face for he knew that snake soup was a delicacy for which he could charge his diners a very high price. Almost as much as what he had been charging his special customers for the dog soup that had resulted from that nice, black cocker spaniel that he had found one night wandering on the beach with no owner in sight.

When he pulled up outside the Ocean Wave Mister Wong walked up the steps - over the still screaming and prostrate Kaye Smith - and took stock of the situation. He decided to attack the creature from behind. Like a Viet Cong in the jungle he slithered along the floor of the deck as silently as his quarry. Then he jumped up and brought the sharp edge of the spade down on to the back of the python's head. It went in deep. Mister Wong then used his strength to push it in further until it sliced right through the powerful muscles and made a small thud on the deck. Then he pulled it out and struck again. There were audible sighs of relief as the guests came to realise that the python was no longer a threat.

As his reward Mister Wong got the fleshy carcass which he took back to the Kowloon Restaurant and chopped it into small pieces before spicing it for the next night's soup.

An ambulance arrived to take Kaye Smith to the hospital for an immediate operation to insert a metal pin and plate in her leg and the photographer rushed back to his newspaper in order to get his priceless action shots on to the front page of the next day's edition. Dick was to get his publicity all right but not in the way he expected. Of course, none of the diners finished their meal and so did not pay their bills.

As a result of the photographs in the paper there were no guests for the next few nights. However, at the week-end a new batch of tourists arrived in town and some of them made their way to the Ocean Wave.

Business began to pick up and Dick was confident enough to start ordering again. The seafood platter was proving very popular - especially with visitors from the southern states who were curious to try the Moreton Bay bugs which were a specialty of the area.

Dick ordered the seafood from various sources and it was delivered in refrigerated trucks. The order for oysters was a separate one and the driver just happened to be one of Ronnie's surfing friends.

Instead of taking the consignment direct from the coolstore to the restaurant, as he had been instructed to do, he decided to make his own contribution to the new restaurant's woes. He took the oysters home and left them out in the hot noonday sun while he had lunch and fed his dog, Doobie. After an hour he put them back in the refrigerated truck and delivered them to the Ocean Wave. By the time he handed them over they were cool again.

That night was the first time that all the diners ordered the same dish - the seafood platter.

And, of course, they all got food poisoning. There was not enough room for everyone in the small toilet so they just stood around the edge of the deck and chundered over the railings. Just like when a ship has a rough passage. Once again, nobody paid their bills and one overweight American woman threatened in the loudest and shrillest of voices to sue Dick for poisoning her.

Word quickly spread and more nights with empty tables followed. However, there was hope on the horizon as the next week-end there was to be an international surf contest at Pineapple Point and people from all over the world were expected to turn up. They would not all be barefooted surfers, reasoned Dick, but administrators, judges, sponsors and people like that who would know how to dress for dinner and who would be only too delighted to eat at such an exotic place where, if the surf was really big, the spray of the contest wave might fall on them as they ate their food.

Imagine his delight when, on the Saturday night, he received a telephone booking from the World Champion himself, an American multi-millionaire sportsman who was also reputed to be a gentleman who presumably would know how to dress for dinner. A special table was prepared and Dick and his wife were fussing around so much that some of the other guests began to wonder if the Queen herself might be coming.

The champion duly arrived in the company of his sponsor and the sponsor's wife. The three of them sat down at the table and looked around at the exotic foliage. Dick, resplendent in a white shirt, black bow-tie and maroon cummerbund, served them some wine and they placed their order.

All went well until a group of young people (all properly dressed) got up and paid their bill. They then drove to the local pub for further lubrication.

Inside the public bar they were quick to boast that they had just seen the World Champion who at that moment was dining at the Ocean Wave. The word spread like a summer bush fire and it was not long before cars and panel vans were starting up and heading for the Ocean Wave. All the groupies who had come to the contest were on their way to mob their idol. There was not a man among them.

They did loud handbrake stops on the newly paved road outside the restaurant and, ignoring the dress code sign at the entrance, they rushed on to the deck and started screaming in ecstasy at the sight of their hero eating his pepper steak. They had been drinking for several hours and were in no mood for restraint. A honey blonde ran up, threw her arms around his neck and started kissing him madly. Another one ripped off her bra and waved it in his face. This was more than the others could bear and there was a wild rush to his table by more than a hundred crazed groupies.

Tables were knocked over in the melee which followed and the other diners, some of them bruised and bleeding, withdrew down the wooden steps. There was even a fight over the champion's half eaten steak. They all wanted it as a souvenir.

Dick grabbed a broomstick and waved it in the air but to no avail. He yelled at them to go away but his voice was drowned out by the high pitched squealing.

Eventually he and the sponsor managed to grab the champion and pull him inside the restaurant where they bundled him into the toilet and locked him in there on his own. At least he was now free from being mobbed and hopefully they would all go away. They did no such thing.

When this all-girl army realised that the target of their desires had been taken away from them they went on the rampage. Everything was smashed - plates, glasses, bottles, windows, tables, chairs, vases. The Vandals themselves could not have done such a thorough job. When there was nothing more to smash inside they went back to the deck and broke every table, chair and piece of crockery. Then they all got back in their cars and drove back to the pub for another drink.

A stunned Dick limped over to the toilet door and unlocked it. The champion walked out and looked around him. It was like the aftermath of a tank battle. "I'm very sorry," he said to Dick and Bella, "but I can not be held responsible for what these mad people do."

"No, of course you can't," said Dick with difficulty.

"No way are we paying for the meal." said the sponsor. "We never even finished it."

"No, of course not," said Dick as he escorted them down the steps of the shattered deck.

Later that night Dick and his wife lay in bed in silent contemplation. "Do you know what I'm thinking?" he asked.

"Probably the same as me," was her reply.

There was a pause for a moment. Dick was the first one to speak. "We ran it for six years without a hitch. We knew all our customers almost as if they were family. We liked them and they liked us. And, if I hadn't listened to that silly upside down Australian flag, we wouldn't have had any of these problems."

"I've just thought of something," she said.

"What?"

"When they fly the flag upside down, it's a sign of distress. Ships do it when they get into difficulties at sea."

"Well, it's certainly been a sign of distress in our case. Let's clean it up and make it into a surfers' bar again."

"What a good idea!"

The restaurant was closed for two weeks while joiners and glaziers repaired all the damage.

When it reopened Dick decided to fly the flag from the high post at the top of the gable. He reasoned that, since the upside down flag had brought such disaster, then the right way up should lead to great success. And so it did. Lower prices, lots of burgers for hungry surfers, rash vests once again hanging over the railings, Dire Straits on the stereo and lots of noise and laughter.

Every morning Dick raised the Australian flag which, with its colourful Union Jack and the stars of the Southern Cross, is one of the most beautiful and meaningful in the world. And every morning, as he ran it up the flagstaff, Bella would say the same words, "Make sure the flag is not upside down!"

CHAPTER TWO

RAVEY DAVEY

The path of true love rarely runs smoothly and that was certainly the case with Davey and Wendy. They first met on the dance floor of a rave club in Swansea where, once you were inside the door, all inhibitions were thrown to the wind.

It began when a huge smoke bomb went off in the middle of the dance floor and visibility was reduced to virtually zero. Davey, a regular raver, had been dancing in a world of his own and had wandered a few yards along the crowded floor from where his girl-friend was.

When the smoke bomb went off he felt like a few moments of intimacy and so, through the thickening smoke, he moved back to where he thought he had left her. It was that time of night when he was feeling very pleasant but also a little confused which probably explains why, when he saw the girl with blonde hair and a short, black satin dress, he put his arms around her and kissed her passionately. He thought she felt a bit different - but so did he. One thing was certain: he'd never had a kiss like this before. But when the smoke started to clear he noticed that the slim and beautiful girl into whose eyes he was now looking was not his girl-friend at all but a total stranger who at that moment looked and felt lovelier than any girl he had ever known.

When his girl-friend saw what had happened, she decided to play tit-for-tat and immediately fell into the arms of a swarthy, Mediterranean looking type who happened to be dancing next to her. "Well," thought Davey, "I suppose that's the type of thing that can happen at a rave. Things can get a little crazy."

Chatting up the new girl was out of the question; the loud thump-thump of the techno precluded it and anyway, what was the point when they had already got to know each other so intimately?

Davey was wearing wide, baggy trousers and his special white disco shirt which glowed under the powerful ultra-violet lights. The old wooden floor was shaking with the stomping of a thousand feet, brightly coloured balloons filled with helium were floating through the air while men dressed as clowns and girls with glitter and silver stars on their faces glided past like graceful swans. But much of this was lost on Davey and Wendy who danced on the same spot for the next three hours in a state of total contentment.

Afterwards they walked to the nearby house of one of Davey's friends for a late night party that was full of wide eyed people and stupid conversation. When the first light of dawn appeared Wendy started to yawn and so Davey, ever the gentleman, offered to drive her home.

He led her along the road to the car-park and that was where she saw his vehicle for the first time. Not a car, not a van, not even a lorry. Davey explained how the local ambulance station had recently taken delivery of a new set of ambulances and had sold off the old ones, one of which he had bought as it was in sound mechanical condition and was big enough for him to put his surfboards and other gear in the back where the patients used to lie and, in some cases, die.

Wendy did not know whether to laugh or cry but at least she didn't mind getting in which, Davey told her, was better than what had happened to one of his surfing mates who had bought an old undertaker's hearse as a camper van and had had great trouble getting any girl to go away with him. "The spirit of the dead bodies and all that sort of thing," explained Davey with a casual wave of his hand.

Wendy had to admit that, among his other qualities, her new beau was certainly interesting. All her previous boyfriends had driven new Fords and Vauxhalls and things like that. When they came to a red light Davey simply turned on the siren and sped through. She could not stop giggling when he explained that, if you look like an ambulance, you might as well behave like one.

They eventually arrived at her large house which overlooked the beach at Mumbles where Davey usually surfed. He wondered why he had never seen her down at the beach but she said that she was usually so busy with her studies that she did not have too much time for leisure. "As a matter of fact, to-night is the first time I've ever been to a rave," she said.

"And what did you think of it?"

"Different."

"Does that mean you'll come out with me next week-end?"

"Yes, but why don't we go somewhere else? A place that's not so loud so that we can have some conversation."

"Good idea. One of my surfing mates owns the seafood restaurant down at the beach. I'll book a table for 8.30 next Saturday."

After that they started to meet regularly. In fact, apart from her study commitments (she was reading Welsh literature at the local university) they found that they couldn't see enough of each other. Wendy even began to wander down to the beach to watch him surf and bit by bit she started to meet his friends and to hang with the surfing crew. But there were problems.

When he was not surfing Davey worked as a cobbler in his father's business in which he was an equal partner. It was a good, honest trade but unfortunately was not nearly good enough for Wendy's parents who were members of the Crachach, that small group of Welsh speaking families who hog all the positions on the cultural and other public bodies that are subsidised by the taxpayer. They seriously believed that Wales could not survive without their precious contribution while the rest of the people - including Davey - thought they were a bunch of snobs.

Wendy's father was a professor of Welsh language and a director of the local Eisteddfod. The first question he asked Davey when he met him was whether or not he spoke Welsh. The tone in which the question was asked spoke more than the words themselves and Davey decided to answer like with like. "No," he replied, "I spend most of my spare time surfing. Do you surf?"

The father made some reply in Welsh which Davey could not understand. It didn't bother him; some of his friends could speak Welsh but they didn't have the attitude problem that this man seemed to have. "Come on," said Wendy, "It's time to get going; otherwise we'll be late."

When they got into the ambulance Wendy apologised for her father's behaviour, explaining that he was a bit of a fanatic with a chip on his shoulder. Davey wondered why a man with a nice, big house, a Jag in the garage and a lovely daughter like Wendy would have a chip on his shoulder.

The more he thought about the rudeness of the father - and, to a lesser extent, of the mother, for she too had laid on the bit about what a great shame it was that Davey hadn't been successful enough at school to go on to university - the more he realised how much he loved Wendy. If he didn't, he would not have put up with the barely concealed hostility to which he was subjected every time he called for her or took her home.

It did not help matters when he bought her a surfboard for her birthday and began to teach her how to ride it down at the beach. "What a frivolous way to spend your time," declaimed her mother who was something big in "public administration".

"Yes, but I enjoy it," replied Wendy. "And anyway, Davey spends so much time down at the beach that I wouldn't see so much of him if I wasn't there too."

"Well, what is his main interest? You or the waves?"

"If I'm down at the beach, he can enjoy both of us at the same time."

"I don't know why you can't meet someone from your classes at university instead of hanging round with a wretched cobbler who drives an old ambulance."

"I prefer to judge people by what they are rather than what they do." And so it went on.

Davey and Wendy went on a surfing holiday to Portugal where, instead of getting on each other's nerves, they found a contentment which persuaded them that they should spend the rest of their lives together. A week after they got back they decided to announce their engagement.

Davey, who was both polite and direct, called on her father one evening and asked for the hand of his daughter in marriage. To that sneering, silver haired snob the request was unwelcome but not entirely unexpected and he realised that he and his conceited wife would have to bow to the inevitable; the alternative, he knew, was that the young couple would run off and get married anyway - which would create a permanent breach between them and their much loved only daughter. So, with as much grace as he could muster and without any show of enthusiasm, he agreed to the proposal and then started asking Davey all sorts of highly personal questions about his sexual background and the state of his bank account. Davey, so happy that his proposal had been accepted, answered politely but not always truthfully.

The wedding was set down for the first Saturday of May at the fashionable church of Saint Quinton. Since they had only one daughter, Wendy's parents decided to turn on a big show to which they invited all the other self-important members of the Crachach. As her father kept saying, " I hope nothing important happens in Wales on the day as there'll be no one around to make a decision; they'll all be at the wedding."

Out of love for his sweetheart Davey was prepared to put up with all the pretentious behaviour, the bouts of rudeness and much else besides. He went out of his way to be co-operative on all counts and didn't even object when he was told that the bride's parents were inviting four times as many guests as the number allocated to his own side.

He even learned some Welsh sentences to include in his wedding speech and he gave strict instructions to the few surfing friends he was allowed to invite to wear suits and ties and to make a special effort to be nice to the bride's parents "who seem to be a bit different from the rest of us".

On the day itself Davey woke up very early. In a state of nervous excitement he started doing all sorts of little chores around the house. The wedding was not until two o'clock but by half past nine he was wondering how on earth he would fill in the next four and a half hours.

Suddenly the telephone rang. It was Nick, his Best Man, who said that he too was feeling nervous and that the biggest swell for a month was rolling into the bay. "Why don't we go for a special pre-wedding surf?" he suggested to the bridegroom.

"Yes, well it would fill in the time," replied Davey. "I've got my speech off pat and my clothes are all ready but I'll have to be back by quarter past twelve in order to have a shower and get ready."

"All right. I'll see you down there in ten minutes."

When he arrived at the beach and saw the powerful and cleanly formed six footers that were breaking so perfectly Davey realised that they were a special wedding gift from Huey and so, still in a highly nervous state, he paddled out and joined the others in the line-up. Nick was there too and some of the others started making a few jokes about getting to the church on time and that sort of thing.

"Your last few hours as a bachelor," called out Nick. "Be sure to make the most of them."

"I am," screamed Davey as he took off on a wave and then ducked low into a barrel. And that was not the only barrel he scored that day. It was one of the best sessions he'd ever had and by the time he looked at his waterproof watch he found that it was almost midday. He decided to paddle out once more for the last wave of his bachelorhood. Then it would be time to go in.

He waited for the next set which was really huge. Nick scored the first wave and then Davey took the second one and went to go left. He could feel the surge of the water picking up his board and driving him on. "Just like we are driven on through life by powerful forces," he thought. "Like love, which is the force behind my appointment at the altar in a couple of hours."

Unfortunately, the wave broke a bit sooner than expected and Davey was thrown by the force of the water at a weird angle. As he floundered around in the swirling sea he could feel that something was very wrong with the back of his neck; he had torn the ligaments and the pain was so excruciating that it was a struggle to stay afloat.

Nick and one or two others saw immediately that something was wrong and they paddled over to where Davey had just retrieved his board. "It's my neck," he screamed above the roar of a breaking wave. They gathered around, lay him on his board and pushed him towards the shore, dodging the incoming waves as best they could.

When they got him to the beach they decided not to waste time calling an ambulance. There was no need; they already had one. Nick unlocked the back of the vehicle and they lay the patient down on the mattress inside.

Nick drove it to the hospital, sounding the siren at intersections or wherever there was heavy traffic. Davey was fully conscious and noted the irony of being driven to hospital in his own ambulance. But he was more concerned with the next couple of hours. The minutes were ticking by and the entire Crachach would soon be arriving at a wedding with no bridegroom. He knew that he would be accused of all sorts of things from deserting his bride on the steps of the altar to selfishness for going for a surf on the morning of his wedding.

His worst fears were realised when they reached the hospital where a white coated doctor took some X-rays and declared that he would have to be operated on immediately.

As he was being wheeled along the corridor to the operating theatre he could hear some music from a radio that was in one of the rooms. It was one of the tunes from My Fair Lady - "Get Me To The Church On Time". By two o'clock he was under anaesthetic.

Right up to the point where the doctor said he would have to operate both Davey and Nick were hoping against hope that somehow all would be well and that they would be able to fix him up in time for the wedding. For that reason they decided not to ring Wendy's house and cause what might well turn out to be unnecessary alarm.

It was ten past one when the doctor put an end to their hopes and Nick was charged with the most unpleasant task that could befall any Best Man - telling the bride that the bridegroom would not be turning up.

He spent a few minutes looking for a pay phone and then a few minutes more waiting for the old lady who was using it to finish her inane conversation. By the time he got through to Wendy's house he was told by the person who had been left to guard all the expensive wedding presents that the bridal party had already left as they wanted to go first to the cemetery where Wendy was to lay some flowers on the grave of her recently deceased grandmother. From there they would be driving straight to the church.

"Have they got a mobile phone in the car?" screamed Nick who was beginning to wish that the floor would swallow him up.

"No. Wendy's father doesn't believe in them. He's a traditionalist, you know."

"Yes, of course," said Nick as he put down the receiver.

He looked at his watch. It was now half past one. The church was about twenty-five minutes away. There was only one thing to do. He would have to go there and give the terrible news in person.

He got back in Davey's ambulance and, with a rev of the accelerator, took off in the direction of the church. He had the siren on the whole way which enabled him to speed through red lights and so he pulled up outside the grey Gothic structure at precisely ten minutes to two. When he turned off the siren he could hear the church bells ringing out from the belfry.

The guests in all their finery were filing into the church. The noise of the siren caused some of them to turn around. These were the types of people who ran the ambulance service but nevertheless looked down their noses at ambulance drivers - especially this one who was wearing only a T-shirt, torn board shorts and bare feet.

A moment later the bride's car arrived and her father jumped out to help her alight. It was a big moment for both of them. However, the happy smile on the bride's face and the smug look of her father soon disappeared when they saw the Best Man run up to them in his surfing gear. His message was blunt and clear. "You'll have to stop the wedding. Davey can't make it. He's in the hospital having an operation."

"Why, what's happened?" snapped the father. "Did he have a car accident?"

"No, it was a surfing accident. It happened in the waves."

"You mean he went surfing on his wedding day?" exclaimed the incredulous father.

"Yes, but it wasn't his fault. It was an accident and anyway, I'm the one who talked him into going for a surf. It's just that the waves were so good."

The father burst into a torrent of abuse that, fortunately for Nick, was in Welsh and so he couldn't understand it. But the look of pure hatred in his eyes was enough to show that he was not uttering words of praise.

Up to this moment Wendy was in a state of shock and could not speak. When she finally came round she started asking questions about how Davey was and what was happening to him. She then announced that she was going straight to the hospital to sit and wait for him to come out of the operating theatre.

In her bridal dress and veil and still carrying her bouquet she walked over to the ambulance with Nick and climbed in. He started the motor and they drove off to the hospital.

The last of the guests, who were just entering the churchyard, looked shocked as they saw the bride running off with a roughly clad surfer in an old ambulance. Things like that just did not happen at these types of weddings and their narrow little minds immediately assumed that the escape in the ambulance meant that the bride must be pregnant and was about to go into labour in which case the unfortunate little baby would miss being legitimate by only a few minutes. What a funny old world it was!

Instead of swanning into the picturesque old church with his daughter on his arm in front of all the Crachach, the father of the bride walked slowly up the aisle with all sorts of confusing thoughts and intentions spinning through his head. What would he tell them? Would they believe it? What would all these precious and socially sensitive people say about it behind his back? Should they still have the reception for which he had paid tens of thousands of pounds to the caterer? Should he tell them the truth that the accident occurred in the waves or would that belittle the standing of his daughter by suggesting that her proposed husband thought so little of her that he went off surfing when he should have been getting ready for the wedding?

It was all too much for the poor man and, when he reached the steps of the altar from where he was to make his announcement, he was struck by a brain tumour and fell down on the stone floor in a comatose state.

There was now neither a groom nor a bride nor the father of the bride. The officiating minister, who was waiting on the altar in his vestments, ran over and began giving the last rites.

The Crachach had been to many society weddings but they had never seen anything like this before. The mixture of farce and tragedy continued when Wendy's mother rushed out of her pew to be with her stricken husband and, in her haste, tripped on the edge of the kneeler and fell flat on her face in the aisle, her big, white hat falling off and spinning towards the altar.

The seriously ill man was taken to the hospital in an ambulance (a real one this time) and was placed in intensive care which meant that the poor bride spent the evening of her intended wedding day going from her fiancé's bed to her father's.

The guests went their separate ways, tut-tutting and gossiping about the scandal of it all. They were more or less equally divided between those who claimed that the bridegroom had done a runner and those (mostly the latecomers who had seen the old ambulance) who swore that the bride was pregnant and had been rushed to hospital to have the baby.

"That's what happens when you get tied up with cobblers and surfers," declared Lady Morris-Davies. "What I wouldn't give to be a fly on the wall at the hospital."

Things at the hospital were slowly improving. When Davey came out of the anaesthetic a few hours later his head felt like lead and he couldn't lift it off the pillow. He soon recognised Wendy, who was still in her bridal dress, and her soft touch helped him return to the world of reality. "Do you still want to marry me?" he asked hesitantly.

"Of course."

"Even though I went surfing on my wedding day?"

"It was an accident. I've always known that I have to share you with the waves. But surfing is a big factor in making you what you are. If you didn't surf you would not be the Davey that I know and love."

"If that's how you feel, we had better get on with it. It seems a shame to be in a wedding dress with nothing happening. Go and find the hospital chaplain and tell him to come up here. And, if Nick is still around, tell him to come up too. I might not be able to move very much but I'm certainly capable of exchanging marriage vows."

Half an hour later the wedding took place in the incongruous setting of the sterile, white hospital room with Davey lying flat on his back in bed and Wendy standing beside him. The only others in the room were the chaplain, the faithful Nick as Best Man and a nurse who had been roped in to fulfil the legal requirement of a second witness.

At the end of the brief service the nurse hurried away as she was on duty and the chaplain, who usually dealt with the dying, produced a bottle of champagne and some glasses. Still feeling the effects of the anaesthetic, Davey would not have any champers as he knew that it would produce a cocktail too far. There had already been enough accidents for one day.

"And how did you two meet in the first place?" asked the chaplain.

"We met in the middle of a smoke bomb at a rave," replied Davey. "I thought she was someone else. You see, I went up to the wrong girl but she turned out to be the right one."

"Ah, the curious ways of the Lord!" exclaimed the chaplain.

"Yes," thought Davey as he lay there with a beam of happiness all over his face. Not only had he married his loved one but, through "the curious ways of the Lord", he had managed to do it without her father or any of his Crachach friends being present.

CHAPTER THREE

THE TWISTS OF FATE

"The loveliest fleet of islands that lies anchored in any ocean".

- Mark Twain on Hawaii

Phil Redwood was nineteen when he first arrived on the Hawaiian island of Oahu in the autumn of 1941. He was a fresh faced, crew cutted young man who had been brought up on his father's cotton farm in the Black Belt of Alabama. However, the collapse of the cotton price during the 1930s Depression and the ruthless behaviour of the banks in cancelling their loans to small cotton farmers in order to protect the big brutes had led to foreclosure, the loss of the Redwoods' home and land and the break-up of the family. That was why Phil had joined the Navy as soon as he left school. He was a machinist in the engineering branch and was currently serving on the battleship, *USS Arizona* which, on this balmy Pacific morning, 7th December, 1941, was at its anchorage with the rest of the Fleet across the water from Waikiki Beach.

Phil enjoyed being in the Navy - the camaraderie, the opportunity to learn a trade and to visit interesting and exotic ports - like Honolulu - plus, of course, the shore leave.

Ah yes, the shore leave; that was the problem of the moment. He looked at his watch; it was exactly 6 a.m. His overnight leave would expire in one hour's time. And he was in the colour party for hoisting the ensign on the deck of the *Arizona* at eight o'clock. In two hours time.

The logistics were not a problem; a taxi ride would take only half an hour. The problem was that he didn't want to go back just yet. Maybe later in the morning but that would be too late. By then he would be on a disciplinary charge of being Absent Without Leave (AWOL). Phil had been in the Navy for three years and he had never gone AWOL. But he had never felt like he did just now.

His last few shore leaves had been in the daytime and, on each occasion, he had made his way to Waikiki and rented a long and heavy surfboard from Harry, the old Hawaiian with the bushy grey beard who sat in front of the Royal Hawaiian Hotel where he conducted his business of hiring outrigger canoes and surfboards to the tourists.

Like most servicemen Phil was fit and strong and he enjoyed paddling out the few hundred yards to the reef where the waves seemed to be forever breaking.

Being a beginner, he had kept to the end of the line and watched the others before having a go himself. At first he kept falling off but it wasn't long before he got the knack of it and, with energy, determination and practice, he steadily improved. He savoured every moment he could spend in the water and surfing soon became an addiction. His life seemed to centre round his shore leaves when he would head for the beach, hire a board and spend as many as six and eight hours in the warm Pacific waves.

He was even on nodding terms with some of the hardy Hawaiians and on one occasion he shared the line-up with the great Duke himself who rode his board with such effortless ease, imagination and style.

But this overnight shore leave that was due to expire in an hour had not been so satisfying. Oh yes, he had done the bars in Hotel Street with his shipmates and there had been women and jazz and dancing but somehow that was not as good as getting out there in the wide ocean and riding those powerful waves.

By now Phil was sitting and smoking a cigarette on the sand in front of the Royal Hawaiian Hotel, the lights from its twin towers shining through the pre-dawn darkness. The only sound was the crashing of the waves. Soon the first light of day began to peep through the darkness and the seagulls started their shrill cry. He felt at one with the beach and ocean. He had been brought up inland - more than a hundred miles from the coast. That was why he found the sea - especially Waikiki with its wonderful waves - so exotic and alluring.

Through the improving light he saw some movement further along the beach. Old Harry, who rented the surfboards, was emerging from underneath an overturned canoe which was his sleeping quarters. Phil watched as the big Hawaiian stood to his full height and arched his back.

"To hell with the colour party," thought Phil. "They can find someone else. I'm going into the waves." He stood up and wandered along to where Harry was staring at the ocean.

"I'd like to be your first customer for the day," said Phil in his slow Southern drawl. "Here are some dimes for a board. Give me the one that I had last time." Harry picked it out and lay it on the sand. "And you'd better loan me a pair of shorts as well. I didn't think that I'd be surfing on an all night leave." Five minutes later he was paddling through the warm, blue water to the reef.

He ducked under the breaking waves to the calm water beyond and then turned his plank around and looked up. It was now fully light and he was the only one in the sea. In front of him lay the swathe of sand of the most famous beach in the Pacific. He could see windows being opened in the line of hotels that rimmed the beach. To his right rose the great, cone shaped landmark of Diamond Head, standing like a sentinel guarding the bay. Through the distant haze on the left he could see Hickam Airfield and behind that lay ninety-six ships of the U.S.Pacific Fleet including his own vessel, *USS Arizona*.

He reflected on the tranquillity of the surroundings and also on the incongruity of it all. Here he was, floating on a surfboard in the peaceful Pacific at the dawn of a new day while in Europe great battles were raging and people were being bombed out of their homes every night. The previous day he had read of a particularly heavy bombing raid on the naval port of Plymouth in Devon. That was where his forebears had come from before they sailed to America at the beginning of the nineteenth century.

Like most people in the South, Phil was of good British stock and his family had never lost their identity with or affection for what they still called "the Old Country". Seventy-five years after the Civil War Phil still preferred the British to the Northern Yankees who had inflicted so much damage on the South both during and after the Civil War. He only wished he could do something to help the Brits in their present plight; they had been stoically taking the punishment from the Nazis for more than two years while America had been sitting back and making lots of money out of selling them ships and planes.

Suddenly he saw a set coming through. He could feel his big board moving underneath him as it was pushed forward by the power of the wave. He paddled for all he was worth and then stood up and experienced that wonderful feeling all over again.

One or two others paddled out to join him but that was all. It was Sunday morning and most Hawaiians were on their way to church.

More and more sets came pounding through and Phil was enjoying it so much that he didn't give a thought to the fate that awaited him when he returned to his ship AWOL. The recklessness of the true surfer.

He had now been in the warm, clear sea for about two hours and the sun had long since risen over Diamond Head. It was going to be another hot, sunny day. He looked out to sea and saw a beautifully formed wave rolling towards him; it seemed to have his name written all over it. He paddled madly and took it just at the right moment. It was a dream ride that seemed to go on forever as the mountain of water kept rolling over the coral. Eventually he wiped out and then stroked his way back to the line-up.

There was a bit of a lull and he could hear the distant drone of engines. He looked up into the cloudless, blue sky and saw formations of aircraft flying in from the north - above the valley that runs between the mountains and which to-day is the Kamehameha Highway to the North Shore. Others were approaching from over the mountains, their wings glistening in the early morning sun. "It's very early on a Sunday for the Air Force to be doing an exercise," he thought.

Phil sat astride his plank and reckoned that he had never seen so many planes in the air at one time. There were almost two hundred - fighters, bombers and torpedo carriers. They started to break up into smaller groups. As they got closer he noticed that all the planes had fixed landing gear and he knew that American planes didn't. Suddenly another formation flew in from the north east and this time he could see them more clearly. Instead of the white star of the American planes they all bore a big red and white circle on their fuselage and wings. The markings of the Japanese Air Force. On they flew towards Pearl Harbour where the battleships of the U.S.Pacific Fleet were lying peacefully at anchor.

"But Japan is thousands of miles away," he thought, "and the United States is not at war with anyone."

He watched aghast as the Zeros dived to attack their unsuspecting target. Loud explosions resonated through the peaceful morning and in the distance he could see flashes of fire and bright light leaping into the air. A few minutes later clouds of thick, black smoke began to rise from "Battleship Row".

His incredulity turned to anger as he thought of his shipmates being bombed from the hitherto peaceful skies by these barbarians from the East. He began to wonder about the colour party.

They did, in fact, find someone to fill in for him and parade on the deck for the daily ceremony. Unfortunately the ensign never reached the top of the flagstaff. It was only half way up when the *Arizona* was hit and everyone on the deck was cut down in a single, searing flash. The bomb set off the forehead magazines and the great battleship was blown apart. A few lucky ones managed to dive from the lower decks into the sea, which was fast filling with oil, and swim to Ford Island or the shore of the base.

Phil hesitated for a moment. Everyone in the line-up had stopped surfing and were sitting or lying on their boards, watching the live display in the distance. "I think the old Hawaiian god of war is breathing fire," declared a corpulent native who was on Phil's left.

Phil could see a set coming through and it looked inviting. Should he surf or should he rush back to help with the casualties? The wave solved his dilemma. He paddled for all he was worth, jumped on his board and rode it as far as it would carry him. It was, he reflected, the last wave of peace. While stroking his way towards the shore he could hear the sirens of the emergency services which were springing into action and speeding towards Pearl Harbour.

As he stepped on to the sand he could see another flight of Zeros that had just arrived over the target and were dropping their loads. He was angry and he knew that such a treacherous and dastardly deed could be avenged only by turning the blue Pacific into a sea of blood. Mostly Japanese blood, he hoped. But at least he was still alive - thanks to the fact that he had gone AWOL in order to have a surf.

He handed his board to Harry, put on his clothes and ran up to Kalakaua Avenue. A fire engine was just setting off so he jumped on its running board and hitched a ride.

With its siren blaring the big red machine picked up speed as it roared along the wide avenue and then turned left into South Beretania Street. On they went - past the old royal palace - and on towards the scene of action.

Everything was in chaos and there was a huge traffic jam for at least a mile outside the main gate of the base. Many vehicles were trying to get in but even more were trying to get out. Delighted with the fear and panic they had caused, the Japs began to strafe the cars on the ground.

Phil jumped off the fire engine and covered the rest of the journey on foot, diving on the ground under a tree every time a menacing plane appeared overhead.

When he eventually got to the landing, from where the launch usually took him back to his ship, he could see the *Arizona* - or at least what was left of it - on fire. It had been his home for many months but was now just a twisted and burning wreck.

By mid morning there was a lull in the bombing as the Zeros were flying back to their aircraft carriers to collect more bombs. Phil joined a rescue launch which was picking wounded and frightened sailors out of the sea and ferrying them ashore to the waiting ambulances. Some were bleeding, some were screaming and some were dead. He worked all day, taking cover every time a new wave of bombers came over and dropped their lethal loads.

By nightfall Battleship Row had become "Battleship Graveyard" and some 2,400 American sailors had been killed. Phil pressed on until he was almost asleep on his feet, bearing in mind that he had been up dancing and drinking all the previous night and had then gone surfing for a couple of hours. He decided to get off the launch the next time it reached the landing steps. The last man he pulled out of the water was a face he knew - his divisional officer.

The poor man had already been rescued once and was put on another ship to receive first aid. When it too was bombed he had jumped into the briny a second time. The bandage over the gash in his chest was coming apart. Phil could see that he was losing blood so he ripped off his own shirt to make a dry bandage.

When he recognised him the officer made an effort to speak. "Ah, Redwood, thank God you're safe. You were AWOL, weren't you?"

"Yes, sir," replied Phil rather sheepishly.

"A woman, was it?"

"No, I decided to have an early morning surf. The waves looked so inviting."

"They saved you. If you'd been on board, you would have been killed. No one survived from the colour party. Our poor, old ship is completely destroyed."

"Well, it's a good thing I went surfing."

"Yes, the twists of fate are kind to some but not to others," said the officer in a faltering voice. Two minutes later he collapsed and died.

That night, as Phil was dropping off to sleep in an outbuilding some distance from the base that was serving as a temporary dormitory, he reflected on the weird way that the waves had saved him from certain death. What he had witnessed while out in the surf was one of the great cataclysmic acts of history. It had brought America into the War, thereby tipping the balance to ensure that the brave and hard pressed British would win in the end. By their treachery the Japs had unleashed a ball of fire that would engulf the whole Pacific, culminating in the atomic bombs on Hiroshima and Nagasaki and their own humiliating defeat. And Phil had been one of only a handful of surfers who had witnessed the whole awesome spectacle from the waves of Waikiki

CHAPTER FOUR

SAGA OF A SURFBOARD

My first memory is of waking up in a shaping bay where some gremlin in a mask was shaving me down in order to give me the "right shape" for some suntanned piece of human flesh to plant his big, flat foot on my deck and drive me down the face of a noisy wave. The gremlin's belly hung over the belt of his denim shorts and the thought did cross my mind that perhaps I should be shaving bits off him in order to make him the right shape.

Of course the shaving hurt me but it wasn't nearly as painful as my circumcision when the blighters chopped a piece out of my deck only a few inches in from my tail for no better reason than to provide them with a groove to tie the bloody leash. The only reason I'm always tied to a hairy ankle in the water is because humans are so clumsy and stupid that they keep falling off their boards and are too lazy to chase us through the water as we try to run away from them on the incoming waves. Don't they realise that I and all my little fibreglass friends like to play in the waves every now and then instead of always being forced to stay near the surfer just like an electronically monitored prisoner on parole?

It didn't use to be like this; an old and wizened ten foot long fibreglass fuzzy once told me that, when he was a young grommet about thirty years ago, no one ever put a leash on a surfboard. The sea was a lot cleaner then too. And there were less surfers in the water. The problem with humans is that the more they develop, the more harmful they become. They have destroyed most of the world's forests and have saturated the fields with the poison of chemical fertilisers; even though the sea covers two thirds of their planet, they have managed to pollute it in its entirety and kill most of the whales and fish along the way. They have even poisoned the atmosphere to such a degree that there is now a growing hole in the ozone layer which removes from them a barrier against the sun's rays which God put there for their own protection!

The surfers who plant their smelly feet on my nice, clean deck keep rattling on about how there is no thrill to match riding a surfboard. If that is so, then why don't they treat me better and give me a bit of space instead of keeping me on the end of a short leash as if I'm some sort of extension of their person like an arm or a leg or the end of a dreadlock? Don't they know that the sea is my favourite element too and that I might like to do my own thing occasionally instead of being treated as nothing more than a means of instant gratification for them just like a condom?

Just who do these humans think they are anyway? They are always banging on about right and wrong and ethics and human rights and yet they are the only species that kill their own kind for anything other than food and, unlike the animals in the jungle, they even kill their young before they come out of the womb. Could you imagine a sow or a she-elephant doing a thing like that? Anyway, I mustn't digress as I've been told that most humans feel uncomfortable and can get very nasty when their own perception of their morality is challenged.

After my painful circumcision and "finishing off" I was placed against the wall, resting on nothing more than my sharp pin-tail - just like a ballet dancer standing on the tips of her toes. The board that was standing next to me was a female and at night, after the fat bellied shaper had locked the place up, we got up to some high old jinks. Being a male, my fibreglass skin started to warm up on the part where my rails were touching those of the slim swallow-tail next to me.

That's another thing about these humans; they think they're so bloody clever at putting a man on the moon and killing each other with cruise missiles and terrorist bombs but they haven't even worked out the sexual proclivities of surfboards. It really is simple; each one of us in the fibreglass family is born either male or female but, when we get in the water, it can all change - backwards and forwards. When a board goes right, it is male but, when it goes left, it is female.

In one surf session we can undergo dozens of sex changes and experience the whole gamut of pleasant feelings but this is something that is beyond the imagination of the silly humans who hardly ever have a sex change and, when one of them does, it involves all sorts of expensive operations, divorce and custody hearings, buying or stealing new clothes and having to send out cards to everyone it has ever known, stating that Mr. John Bull now wishes to be known as Miss Jane Cow.

What happy nights we spent leaning against the wall of the shaping bay! One night things got so hot that the end of my pin-tail seemed to stretch until it was hardly touching the floor. Crash! Down I went, taking my hot, sweating, female neighbour with me. We were at it all night but had a rude awakening the next morning when the shaper with the fat belly opened the big sliding door and saw that we had moved from the vertical position against the wall to the horizontal position on the ground.

He screamed out a number of one syllable words (every one of them containing only four letters) before picking us up and checking to see if any of our fibreglass skin had been broken. It hadn't but it was still hot from all the shenanigans of the night. Then, do you know what the silly bugger did? He stroked the hairs on his chin (shapers rarely shave) and then a few pieces of grey matter must have moved inside his big head as I saw him walk over to his desk and pick up the telephone book.

He then rang the number of the Earthquake Institute to ask if there had been an earthquake during the night. When they told him "No" he merely shook his head and stroked the stubble on his chin again.

Gee, I thought, with brains like that it's a good thing he's a surfboard shaper and not a rocket scientist. And all because his human imagination does not extend to the possibility that surfboards might have sex lives and like a bit of a party.

Anyway, that was the end of our little "romp in the hay" as it were and later that day I was separated forever from the hot, little lady swallow-tail who had introduced me to the pleasures of sex at such an early age by giving me such a great time the night before.

Somebody who must have been important came into the surfboard factory shortly after lunch and started to pick each of us up and look us over as if we might have some contagious disease. I really didn't like the vibe that this chap gave out and, when he picked me up, he banged me down again, claiming that I was "too thick in the rails". Well, I can tell you that, if I had arms, I would have punched him on his suntanned little nose. Who is he to speak like that about me? He wasn't very good-looking himself and obviously had ugly eyes as why else would he cover them with sunglasses when he was inside a building? However, like me, he fell for the beautiful swallow-tail, put it under his arm and walked out of the factory after handing over some coloured pieces of paper which the fat bellied one would probably spend on more beer so that his belly could hang even lower over his belt. If I had a voice, I would have suggested that he use some of the coloured paper to buy a razor.

Always shaving me and my friends down but never himself.

That night I was lonely and cold and was missing the beautiful swallow-tail terribly. I really wanted to get out and see a bit of the world.

Imagine my delight when, at the end of the next day, the one with the fat belly lifted me up and put me in the back of something on wheels which was soon speeding through the countryside. There were six of us altogether in the back of the wagon and I was on top. Now get those ideas out of your mind. The one under me was another male and, unlike some of the crazy, mixed-up and self-indulgent humans, we in the surfboard species are not attracted to our own sex.

The real advantage of being on top was that I was high enough to see out of the windows. Parts of the scenery were very beautiful. Green hills and trees and birds and horses and high cliffs and sandy bays and blue water. But, of course, humans had had nothing to do with all that. Their contribution was grey concrete and telephone wires and black fumes spurting out of their dangerous cars and drunks rolling out of pubs. When I saw what a mess they'd made of it, I counted my lucky stars that I had been born a surfboard and not a human.

Eventually we reached our destination which was a surf shop overlooking the ocean. Inside were lots of pretty things like stylish clothes and coloured magazines, a mountain of white wax, some skateboards and a row of black wetsuits that looked like the Ten Little Nigger Boys without their heads. There were polished tiles on the floor and a video on the wall that showed surf films all day and lots of loud music blaring out of a stereo. Quite an improvement on the dark, old surfboard factory! And the way that the young lads skateboarded into the shop made it seem like one long party.

The owner, whom everyone called Twelve Foot Tim, was a real gentleman. When we were all inside the shop he handed another bundle of coloured paper over to the fat bellied one (whose whole life seemed to revolve around collecting all this pretty paper). We were all leaning against a wall and Tim stood in front of us stroking his chin just like the fat bellied collector of coloured paper except that Tim's chin didn't have any hairs on it. If he was going to have shaved down boards in his shop, he at least had the decency to shave himself. What's sauce for the goose is sauce for the gander and all that.

Eventually, after much stroking of the chin, he said to us out loud, "No, I don't want you there; you'd be better on the other wall." By talking to us he was treating us almost like humans which is all right as far as it goes so long as we don't start to behave like humans.

He didn't do anything that night but the next morning he moved us ever so gently to the other wall which was the best position in the shop as we could see both the video and the changing room which was always being used by well-shaped girls who handed over lots of pieces of coloured paper for the tiniest bikinis and g-strings. Now, I know I'm only a surfboard but I did wonder why they were so willing to part with all those precious pieces of paper for such tiny pieces of fabric when it really wouldn't have made much difference if they had worn nothing at all. Unlike the humans we surfboards are naked all the time except when we're travelling and they put us in a cover.

From time to time people would come into the shop and look at me and pick me up and touch me in all sorts of weird places and then ask Tim how many pieces of coloured paper they would have to give him in order to take me away.

All this was demeaning to say the least. Just like a slave market where the buyers walk along the row, grab the jaw of each slave and then look at his teeth to see if he would be a good buy.

After a couple of weeks I was taken away by a purchaser who, in my humble surfboard opinion, was a complete drongo. He took me into the freezing water and started riding me to the right. Then we went left. Perhaps it was the excitement of my first sex change but, acording to him, I just did not perform to his satisfaction. He wiped out and was dragged under the wave. Ouch! The sharp pull of the leg-rope hurt me in my most sensitive part. The place where I'd been circumcised. What barbarians these humans are!

After emerging from the salty foam, he climbed back on to my deck and started cursing and blaming me for his wipe-out. If I had a voice I would have told him that a good workman should never blame his tools but this drongo wasn't even a good surfer let alone a good workman. Then, at the end of his diatribe, he hit me with his fist. "How dare you hit a woman!" I thought (for I was still female as the last ride had been left).

The next few rides (all left) were better for him and he calmed down a bit but he never apologised for hitting me.

When we were back on the beach he threw me down on the sand like a piece of dirt. "What an ungrateful bastard," I thought. "Out in the water I gave you some good rides and some thrills; without me, you would have been just swimming around in the cold ocean like the drongo that you really are. Surfing consists of three things: the board, the rider and the wave and all three of them must be in harmony for the thing to work."

It happened the very next day when the swell was even bigger. The drongo lay down on top of me and started paddling out and I don't mind telling you that, even through a wetsuit, I could tell that he hadn't showered that morning. As on the previous day he rode me left and he rode me right and, to tell you the truth, I was starting to enjoy all the sex changes. Male one minute and female the next.

The problem with surfers is that they treat us as objects for their pleasure instead of having consideration for our feelings as well. A surfboard is like a wife and, when husband and wife don't get along together, the relationship turns sour. So too with surfboards. There was obviously a serious problem between me and the drongo and, when I saw him take a mouthful of salt water and then spit it out on my nose, I decided that I had had enough.

On the next ride we went close to the rocky point and the invisible underwater eyes that all surfboards have on each side of their nose were able to detect a sharp, steeple shaped rock sticking up from the jagged sea-bed. In the direction that the drongo was steering I was set to miss it by an inch but, unbeknown to the rider, I pulled myself to starboard with just enough force to skim the top of the rocky steeple. The force of the impact threw the drongo into the water and he hit his face on the top of another submerged rock that was shaped like a dome. The architecture down there was really quite ecclesiastical. When he emerged out of the briny he had a gash on the side of his face which was trying to colour the sea red. He started screaming out the same four letter words that I had last heard in the shaping bay when the fat bellied one discovered me on the floor with the swallow-tail.

I came out of it with only a small graze in the rails which hurt a little bit but the pain was well worth it to teach him a lesson.

When we got back to the beach he threw me down on the sand, kicked me in the groin (not far from where I was circumcised) and said that I was "the most useless piece of shit" he'd ever ridden.

I was taken to the ding repairer and patched up and, as far as I was concerned, I was now fightin' fit and rearin' to get back in the water. But, oh no. The drongo decided that he was too good to ride a board that had been broken and so he sold me to another surfer on the beach who was called Dave. Instead of picking me up and banging me down again like all the rude customers used to do in the shop, Dave put a friendly hand on me and said to the others that he was dying to try me out in the water. He had a big smile on his face and was obviously a sensitive surfer who understood the true relationship between rider and board. He put on his wetsuit and out we went. And what a time we had!

Dave and I got along famously; he treated me well and I gave him some really great rides in return. Karma. That's how it works in the surfboard world. So stoked was he that he even gave me a name which, for a surfboard, is really something. My name was "Gecko". Why don't more riders give a name to their boards? Even dogs have names and surfboards, which give so much pleasure to their owners, should not be treated worse than dogs.

Dave was kind to me and kept me in his bedroom when we weren't in the water together. We even had a party one night and he invited all his surfing mates and their spunky looking girl-friends. Most of the chaps I recognised from the line-up and so I didn't have to be introduced to them. There was music and dancing and smoking and drinking and laughter and it was the best vibe I've ever felt. Everyone was cool to me and the sweet smelling smoke in the bedroom made me feel mellow. Dave was sitting on the floor with some of the others when suddenly he looked up at me with a warm smile. "Gee, Gecko, I hope you're enjoying yourself. You and me are the best combination in the bay. You're less trouble than a woman and you give me more pleasure."

CHAPTER FIVE

A VIOLATION OF NATURE

Carl and his wife, Susie, had lived on top of the cliff above the surfing beach of Justowan on the rugged west coast of Cornwall for more than ten years. From the living room of their old, stone walled cottage, which used to be an almshouse, they could look down at the wild waves that rolled in from the North Atlantic. On days when they were rideable Carl was always in the line-up with a handful of other locals.

Although he had two jobs his working hours were flexible. In summer he was busy shaping boards for all those surfers who came down from Bristol and the Midlands to surf some of Britain's best waves but in winter, when the demand for surfboards fell away, he spent most of the time attending to the crops on his two acres of rolling and fertile land. He grew vegetables organically and sold them to nearby restaurants, shops and, of course, friends and neighbours. Carl was a bit of a romantic and looked with wonder on the world as if it was some sort of fairyland. He was also the best surfer in the bay.

Susie had been a schoolteacher before they married and now she spent her time teaching their two young children, Ben, aged nine, and Amanda, seven. She followed the home teaching syllabus and the advantages for the children were that they received a better education and flexible hours so that Ben could surf far more often than if he was a victim of regular school hours. The result was that he was the hottest grommet in the bay.

Every time Carl went for a surf he felt at one with nature; he didn't just love the sea, which gave him so much pleasure, but also the beach and the cliffs and the rolling fields behind that he could see when he was out in the line-up. Every surf he had was special and unique and, at the end of a session, he always picked up something from either the sea or the beach to remind him of that particular surf. Some days he would pick up a piece of floating driftwood, other days a stone or a shell. Once it was a slab of marble that must have fallen off a ship, another time it was a rusty old mine - one of the many that had been laid off the coast in 1940 to prevent a German invasion.

After one of the best surfs he'd ever had, he spotted an old silver coin that was peeping up from under the sand and so that was his souvenir for the day. It was a Queen Mary Silver Groat bearing the date 1554.

When he started picking up all these pieces of memorabilia he would place them at the foot of the round headed Celtic cross at the back of his house - rather like piling an offering on a shrine. The cross dated from the fifth century and marked a place to pray by the wayside for those wandering saints who came to Cornwall from Wales and Ireland and used to walk around the countryside preaching the word of God and doing good works.

After a while there were so many "offerings" that they reached to the top of the cross and, after 1500 years, it was in danger of developing into a shapeless pile. It was then that he acceded to his wife's suggestion that it was time to remove all these things that had been picked up from the beach.

However, since each item represented a happy session in the waves, he could not bring himself to dump them or even to return them all to the beach. Instead, he decided to use the hundreds of pieces to build a modern version of the old Hawaiian "canoe house" where the master board builders (who were usually the chiefs) not only repaired their canoes but also, with their fine adzes and coral sanding blocks, would shape great wooden planks into rideable objects and then polish them with stones to give a smooth finish before staining them with vegetable dye.

Unlike the Hawaiians, who built these open sided structures right on the beach, Carl decided to build his in a grove of trees in the little valley behind the cliffs so as to be sheltered from the fury of the Atlantic gales. Also, he did not want to detract fom the natural landscape - not like the ugly corrugated iron barn on the spur of the hill behind, which stood out like a sore thumb. Everyone in the area thought it was a visual abomination and even the farmer who owned it said that he hated it and would one day pull it down.

Having selected the site and measured out the "canoe house" so as to give him enough space for a shaping bay and storage area, he laid the foundations and dug holes for the wooden beams that would provide the framework of the structure. Then he filled in the gaps with the driftwood and other material that he had collected after each surf. The rusty old mine was built into the foundations while the Queen Mary Silver Groat was specially embedded in the doorstep as a good luck charm. From start to finish it was a labour of love as Carl carefully selected each piece and put it in what he thought was its right place.

The result was that, when he was shaping boards in what he called his "canoe house", Carl was surrounded by four walls that contained a visible reminder of every time he'd been for a surf in the bay. He had usually chosen a piece of driftwood for its interesting shape, or a fine looking shell, which was why the walls, besides appearing unusual, were also beautiful in their own way.

He was forever adding to it and so was young Ben who sometimes spent a long time after coming out of the water in search of just the right memento. It was an eccentric custom but they weren't harming anyone and they were cleaning the beach at the same time. They were just nature lovers trying to surround themselves with nature's gifts in the same way that they revelled in that other gift of nature - the waves.

All went well until the spring of 1999 when the local council decided to charter an expensive aircraft to fly over every inch of the county to snoop on the citizens and take detailed photographs of their land and houses. The country roads were full of potholes, the signposts needed repainting and some of the schools were short of textbooks but the council could still find the funds for hundreds of hours of expensive aerial photography. Snooping on the public was considered far more important than providing them with services.

The first thing that Carl knew of what was going on was one day when he came out of the water, picked up a pale pink tortoise shell to squeeze into some part of the wall, and made his way up to the canoe house. And it was there that he saw a thin, grey haired man, wearing dark trousers and a white shirt and tie, taking photos of the walls. Carl did not think anything of it as quite a few of the neighbours and even some tourists dropped in from time to time to look at and admire his unique creation.

"Are you Carl Abbotson?" the man demanded in the rude tone of officials who have a little bit of power and want the rest of the world to know it. Although he'd only asked a simple question, alarm bells started ringing inside Carl's head for he knew that ordinary people would not have spoken in such a threatening way. The man was obviously looking for trouble.

"Yes," replied Carl politely. "What can I do for you?"

"Did you get a building permit from the council to put up this monstrosity?"

"It is not a monstrosity. It is the most earthly building on the coast. It's all been made of natural things like driftwood and shells. Furthermore, it has special significance for me and my son as it is a living reminder of every time we've surfed in the bay."

"I'm not interested in that crap. Did you get a building permit?"

"I did not think it was necessary. After all, it's hidden in a grove of trees - not like that unsightly barn on Farmer Briggs' land."

"Then I take it that you don't have a building permit in which case it must be pulled down."

Carl could hardly believe what he was hearing. "Well, can't I just be given one? You can see that it is soundly built. The foundations go down nearly three feet."

"You could apply for a permit but, since you have committed a breach of the law by putting up a structure without permission, the council would be unlikely to accede to your request. Since I am the building inspector I would have to make a report; the council nearly always acts on the recommendation of the inspector and there's no way I'd recommend a permit for this heap of shit." He kicked a piece of driftwood with his boot and it fell away.

Carl was livid at such an act of sacrilege and felt like punching the little man in the face but he knew that that would only make matters worse.

"Have you ever built anything yourself?" asked Carl, "because, if you have, you would know how much work - and even love - goes into it and you wouldn't have shown your disrespect by kicking it."

"Listen, laddie, I'm an inspector - not a bloody builder."

"So you've never had any experience of building?"

"No, of course not. I've always been above working with my hands." He was speaking the truth for he was a member of that tyrannical class of petty bureaucrats who spend their entire working lives bossing other people around. Before he was a building inspector he was a tax inspector and before that a safety inspector. If he had been alive in Hitler's Germany he would have made an ideal inspector for the gas ovens, checking them each morning to make sure they were in perfect working order to burn their daily quota of Jews. And he would have done that task just as coldly and efficiently as he was performing his present one of terrorising any citizen who might have committed the unpardonable crime of putting up a small workshop without a wretched permit.

Carl had to go through the bureaucratic rigmarole of applying for the required piece of paper and paying the non-returnable fee. As soon as they got the fee the council lost no time in refusing the permit and Carl was given fourteen days to demolish the structure.

Not surprisingly, he could not bring himself to commit such an act of vandalism. To him it was more than a structure where he worked; it was part of his heart and soul. Every piece of the curious looking walls was a reminder of a particular surf.

It was mid-morning when they came. Carl was in the process of shaping a mal for one of the locals and Susie was explaining past participles to Ben and Amanda in the parlour, which they used as a classroom.

They all ran to the gate when they heard the loud clanging noise of the bulldozer being rolled down the ramp of the big articulated lorry. Then a fat slob with tattoos all over his flabby arms drove it on to their property, knocking down the gate post as he passed.

This was too much for Susie, who knew just how much of himself Carl had put into his beloved "canoe house"; she threw herself down in front of it and forced the great, lumbering piece of metal to come to a halt.

The inspector was furious as, like all officials, he liked everything to proceed smoothly and by the book. And anyway, he had three more buildings (two of them houses) to knock down the same day and he wanted to get on with things. By now Carl and the two children had joined her and all four were lying on the muddy ground.

"Get up this minute!" ordered the inspector.

"We'll lie on our own property if we want to," retorted Carl.

"You are breaking the law by obstructing a council official in the course of his duty." But no one moved.

"If you lay one hand on us, you're a dead man," hissed Carl. He was then reminded - chapter and verse - that it was a serious criminal offence to threaten a council officer in the execution of his duties. Both he and Susie marvelled at how many laws there always seem to be to support Authority and how few there are to protect the citizen.

There was still no movement from the family on the ground, who were trying with their own bodies to prevent an act of wanton vandalism. The inspector had had enough so he rang the police on his mobile phone and summoned them to a "serious breach of the peace".

Two constables arrived and spent some time listening to the inspector quoting all the sections and sub-sections of the various council ordinances that were allegedly being broken. Then they walked over to the prostrate family and, without any enthusiasm, asked them to get up so as to enable the bulldozer to get on with its work of destruction.

"We're staying here." declared Carl. "This is our property for which I paid a lot of hard earned money. The structure is quite safe and is not hurting anyone. It can't even be seen from the road or the beach - not like that ugly barn of Farmer Briggs which is the local eyesore. So, why can't you leave us alone? All we want to do is live our own lives and surf."

Since it was obvious they were not going to move, the cops took off their jackets and started pulling them out of the way. Carl first, then Susie and then the children who were both crying their eyes out and wishing the hell that all these unwanted intruders would go away and let them get on with their lessons so that they could go surfing in the afternoon.

The inspector and his men took everything out of the canoe house and then the bulldozer ploughed into its walls and knocked it to pieces in only a few minutes. All around was scattered driftwood, broken shells and split stones. Dust was rising from the ground and it looked like the aftermath of an earthquake. But at least the structure was flattened and the inspector and his fellow vandals could move on to terrorise their next victims.

A devastated Carl went surfing with Ben later in the afternoon but, when they came out of the water, they just walked up the beach without seeking anything to remind them of their time in the waves. What was the point?

At the end of the day some of the neighbours called in to express their sympathy and to state their views of council officials in fairly robust language. One of them was old Farmer Briggs who said that he thought it was a great shame to destroy such an interesting looking building.

"I just wish they'd bring their bulldozer up and knock down that ugly barn of mine," he said. "I never use it now and its such a blot on the landscape."

"Then why don't you knock it down yourself?" asked Susie.

"I'm not allowed to. The Government has given it a Grade Two listing. It's now officially a listed building that must by law be preserved forever. They told me that it's one of the best examples of 1960s barn architecture in this part of the country. Hard to believe, isn't it? Just a whole lot of sheets of corrugated iron banged together."

Carl was incredulous. "There's certainly no justice in this world," he said sagely.

"Have you only just found that out, young man?" said Farmer Briggs

CHAPTER SIX

THE SEARCH FOR EXCITEMENT

To see twenty-five year old Todd Cronin walking into his advertising office, which was in the shadow of the tall towers of Truro Cathedral in Cornwall, one would think that there went a steady young man with his head screwed on in the right way and a promising future ahead of him. Good looking, well groomed, finely cut suit, old school tie and the type of ready smile that one would expect from an advertising executive who has been trained to smile at all times in front of the client but especially when things go wrong. Rather like a monkey that smiles the most when it is angry. But inside that outwardly steady head there boiled a seething cauldron of dissatisfaction with the superficial path that his life - and especially his job - seemed to be taking.

He could see through the whole sham of advertising and did not want to spend the rest of his life deceiving the public for the benefit of his well-paying clients. He was still only an employee of the firm but the time was fast approaching when he would be asked to be a partner. What would he say?

"Ah, Todd, can I see you for a moment in my office?" said the managing director who put his head through the door of the room where Todd sat at his minimalist style desk.

"Certainly, sir," replied Todd who got up and followed the great man into the holy of holies.

The manager sat down, lit a cigar and said, "Last night we had a partners' meeting and Mr. Petherick announced that he is leaving us to take up a position in London. In conformity with our longstanding policy of promoting talent from among the younger executives it is my pleasure to tell you that, by unanimous decision, the rest of us invite you to become a partner." He looked for the sudden beam that always spread across a young man's face whenever he uttered those magic words but it wasn't there. Worse still, Todd seemed to betray a slightly troubled look.

"Your earnings will be more than doubled," said the manager in an effort to put some icing on the cake. "You will accept, won't you? No one has ever turned us down yet. It is not the type of thing that is offered to many chaps of your age."

"Look, I really appreciate the confidence you've shown in me but it's a big step and I'd like the chance to think it over."

Think it over! No one had ever done that before. Usually they accepted before the manager had even finished his sentence.

"Oh, all right then. I'll give you until to-morrow morning."

As he left the office at the end of the day Todd did not go for a drink with his mates at the half-timbered pub as he usually did. Instead, he sought a quiet spot to think things over. And what better place than the cathedral, the main doors of which were only a few yards in front of him?

Inside the great Gothic structure shafts of twilight were beaming through the stained glass windows and there were a few people waiting for an Evensong service.

Todd found a dark corner, surrounded by a forest of tall pillars, and sat down on one of the polished wooden pews and tried to think things out - hopefully with Divine Guidance. "Lord, please put some excitement into the dull routine of my life."

He thought about his job and how much he hated it. The money was certainly good but the work itself was deeply unsatisfying. Having to think up childish jingles and slogans in order to sell other companies' crap products was not what he wanted to do for the rest of his life. "If I'd wanted a career in brainwashing other people, I should have joined the Soviet secret police," he thought.

He then contemplated how much he looked forward to the week-ends when he spent countless hours riding the waves that are born in Atlantic storms and throw themselves on the Cornish coast. The more he thought about it, the more he realised how wide was the gulf between the pleasure of his week-ends and the boredom and dissatisfaction of his Monday to Friday existence. And now they wanted to make him a partner! More money. And more responsibility. Why, the partners usually worked on

Saturday mornings and then went to golf together in the afternoon. Good-bye to surfing Saturdays! No way José. But what was he to do? The offer of a partnership had brought matters to a head. A decision had to be made which would affect the course of his life. If he refused the offer, he could hardly stay on there but, he decided, he didn't want to anyway. What was the point of having all that money in the bank and being totally unhappy? It was time to spend some of it - on a surfing trip.

Thus it was that Todd walked out of the doors of the air conditioned terminal building at Manila Airport, with his two surfboards and a bag of clothes on a trolley, into the stifling heat and pollution of one of the most chaotic cities on the planet.

He was immediately accosted by dozens of screaming Filipino taxi drivers, one of whom grabbed his boards and bag from the trolley and threw them into the back of a taxi truck. Todd decided that, if he didn't want to lose his gear, he'd better get in too.

For the next three days he stayed in a small hotel overlooking Manila Bay - to get over the jet lag and to make his acquaintance with the Philippines, one of the Orient's most backward countries, and its friendly, smiling people.

The problem with the Philippines was that it had the misfortune of being colonised by the Americans who, lacking the light touch and centuries old experience of other colonising powers like

Britain, France and Portugal, made a complete hash of it. As a result of American inexperience and heavy handedness thousands of Filipinos were killed by U.S. troops while big American companies took everything out of the country that wasn't bolted down.

The American legacy was to leave the Philippines in an impecunious and chaotic state, something which was not improved in later years when local dictators did their worst as well. And the result of all this misfortune? A race of people who are forever smiling as they try to make the most of what they are left with. Singing and dancing is what they live for - as Todd found out when he reached his destination: San Mateo.

It was a small resort at the end of the sprawling island of Luzon and seemed to be what he was looking for - an exotic location, good waves, fine beach, lots of fresh lobster and barracuda, friendly natives and a few Western travellers for company.

By day he surfed the reef - just him and a couple of Germans, Kurt and Wolfgang, who were surprisingly good surfers in view of the fact that they come from a country with hardly any coastline. But, as they explained to Todd, with their generous holidays (six weeks paid leave a year) plus another month of unpaid leave, they were able to spend almost a quarter of the year in sunny climes and surf as much as they liked.

The three of them became good friends, surfing by day and sipping the local brew, San Miguel, in the evenings with some blonde girls from Germany who, instead of surfing, spent all day sunning themselves on the beach. Late at night they would all sit under the coconut palms, listening to the happy Filipinos playing their guitars, and join in the sing-song. It was a very laid back spot - far from the worries and cares of the world.

On the few waveless days Todd and the other surfers joined the girls in the sun and they filled the time playing cards and backgammon and talking about this and that and nothing at all.

The girls liked to sunbathe topless, which was no big deal to anyone - neither Westerners nor locals - until a passing tourist bus of elderly Japanese men happened to make a refreshment stop one afternoon when Todd had just lost a game of backgammon to Ingrid.

As soon as these old men saw the naked breasts of the white girls they started giggling and pointing like a bunch of excited schoolboys about to have their first cigarette. Then they grabbed their cameras and zoom lenses and started taking photos. All the money they had paid for their trip was now worthwhile.

Most of them stood on top of the dunes to get their shots but others couldn't control themselves and rushed down on to the sand to get close-ups. There was a large piece of seaweed on the sand so Todd picked it up ever so casually and hurled it at the face of the most persistent of these emotionally immature pests. It covered his face completely; in fact, it looked so funny that Wolfgang grabbed his own camera and started taking photos of Little Mister Seaweed. But not the Japs, whose lenses remained firmly fixed on nothing but breasts and nipples. Fortunately there was some more seaweed lying around from the big tide of the previous day so they all started to pick up big bunches of kelp and throw them at the cameramen. Unfortunately, raw seaweed is quite a delicacy in Japan and having large amounts of it thrown over one's nose and mouth was not at all uncongenial so Todd and the others started throwing handfuls of sand and this was really effective as no Japanese likes to get sand in his expensive camera. The still giggling old men scampered back to their bus like little boys caught in the act.

Apart from the waves, this mild confrontation was one of the few excitements of a place that was certainly relaxed and exotic but, for Todd, was starting to become dreary. Even Paradise can get boring at times. When Wolfgang flew back to Hamburg, Todd persuaded Kurt to go further south in search of new and hopefully bigger waves.

They crossed the water on an old ferry and then made their way down the island of Samar where they stopped off at a couple of places to surf, but not for long as the urge to see what sort of wave was around the next headland drove them further south.

They sailed on an outrigger to the island of Babak where they hired a jeep and forced it over roads that were unpaved and full of holes as well as being home to straying cows, clucking hens and weird looking dogs.

They spottted a few good waves as they made their way down the eastern coast, facing the Pacific, but for one reason or another (usually lack of accommodation) they decided not to stay. The track they followed had a virgin rain forest on one side and the blue Pacific on the other. The only people they came across were a few roaming aboriginals, whose only attire was a small penis sheath made out of soft animal skin. A far cry from the buttoned up shirts and ties of the advertising office back in Truro. Todd wanted adventure and that was what he was getting.

They reached a bay with near perfect waves breaking off a rocky point and decided to stay. No crowd problems here.

Anchored in a muddy stream were four junks and, by means of sign language and a handful of Filipino money, they scored one of them for their accommodation. Part of the deck was covered by a canopy which provided some much needed shade from the burning sun.

The waves that broke so cleanly and consistently off the point were generous with their barrels and the two adventurous surfers rode them for hours on end. Far out in the turquoise sea they could see an outer reef with a lot of white water crashing over it.

As they sat at night on the afterdeck of their floating lodgings, smoking the local ganga and absorbing the mysteries of the Eastern night, they discussed the prospect of paddling out to the distant reef. Kurt declined on the grounds that the paddle out would be too long and exhausting and anyway, he was thoroughly enjoying the barrels of the point break.

"All right, then, I'll go on my own," declared Todd. "No way am I going to come this far and not check out a gem like that."

The next morning he said good-bye to Kurt and began his mammoth paddle through the crystal clear sea in the direction of that alluring white water. It was a hell of a long way but the hairs on his head tingled with excitement and anticipation as the thunder of the waves breaking over the shallow coral grew louder and louder.

Todd paddled round the reef and then took off on a monster wave that held up for more than two hundred yards as it sped across the submerged coral. When he ducked into the tube it was completely hollow inside and he hardly got a drip on him. It was, he decided, the best wave he'd ever ridden and well worth the long and exhausting paddle out. When it was over he tapped his board and thanked it for its perfect performance. He decided there and then to keep the board forever as a memento of his magic ride.

Todd started to stroke his way out again in an effort to repeat the experience. Unfortunately, the bright sun, that had warmed his back in the morning, had disappeared and black clouds were darkening the sky. He heard some distant thunder. Real thunder. Not the roar of the surf. Then some lightning and some more thunder. The wind was already starting to cut the sea up rough. Not too bad but the waves were now choppy - so unlike that wave of his life that he had taken half an hour earlier. "Looks like there is a good old tropical squall on the way," he thought. "Perhaps I'd better paddle back in. It seems a long way to come for only one wave - but worth it all the same." He turned his board around and resumed the paddling motion as he headed towards the shore.

After a while the wind became really strong and the salty foam was blowing in all directions. The light became so poor that he could no longer see the shore and the tree covered hills behind it but he kept paddling in what he thought was the right direction. At least it was not cold and, so long as he stayed on his board, he thought he would be all right.

Todd could feel a powerful current which seemed to be growing by the minute and he soon realised that he was wasting his time trying to paddle against it. So he put his hands on the rails and did "go with the flow" - like a raft on the Mississippi. He reckoned (rightly) that it was taking him not out to sea but further south down the island and he prayed that he might hit a headland or some other promontory jutting out from the land.

It was not until the late afternoon that his prayers were answered. Through the dim light he could see what looked like palm trees lining a small beach. Eureka! Yes, they were palm trees.

He began paddling madly and he knew from the speed with which his board was now moving that he was out of the treacherous current. A few minutes later he hit the soft sand of the beach. His ordeal was over. Or so he thought.

He looked around for signs of life but there weren't any so he walked to the top of the sand and sat down utterly exhausted. A few minutes later he nodded off into the world of dreams.

Todd awoke with a start when he felt something touch his foot. When he opened his eyes he saw that he was surrounded by several primitive tribesmen with long, straggly, black hair who were carrying spears and long knives. These ones were completely naked and three of them had bones through their noses. They reminded him of some stuffed models he had once seen in the Natural History Museum.

Strange, surly and suspicious, they motioned him to stand up. One of them picked up his surfboard and started examining it with great thoroughness, tapping it and running his hand over it as if he was expecting something magical to happen.

With the sharp point of a spear touching the bare skin of his back, Todd was marched a short distance through the trees to a small hut made of dried branches.

He sat down on the dusty floor of the hut while the tribesmen talked among themselves in a strange dialect and made various signs with their long, thin hands. Todd reckoned they were trying to decide what to do with him. Then began another inspection of the surfboard. One of them tapped a message on it and then put his ear to the board for a reply.

It was the feast day of the god of fire and, if they did not give him a powerful enough offering, he would be so angry that he would burn their tree huts. So, what was it going to be? The white man or the white surfboard? Both had come out of the ocean and an offering of something from the sea was the most valuable offering of all.

Todd could see them staring at him with their weird looking eyes and it made him uneasy. He thought back to when he had sat in Truro Cathedral and begged the Almighty for a bit of excitement in his life. But now his prayers were being answered to excess so he began to pray the other way - for a little less excitement and some safety. Even dullness!

They picked up the white surfboard and led Todd out of the hut and into the inky blackness of the night. He could still feel the sharp point of the spear touching his sweating back. In front of him walked two young women carrying the surfboard on their heads.

They walked deeper into the jungle until they came to a small clearing, in the middle of which was a broken down pile of big stones that was apparently their temple. From the other side of it Todd could hear a sound that was part chanting and part wailing.

There must have been a hundred men and women around the shrine although, in the pitch darkness, Todd could see only the whites of their eyes and teeth. The black magic ceremony was about to begin.

Fortunately for Todd the last time they burnt a human (a Japanese trader who had entered their territory looking for sea cucumber) had not been a success as the next day there had been an electric storm where the lightning set fire to the forest. Perhaps the flat, white object with the smooth surface and the strange thing sticking out of it, which looked like the dorsal fin of a shark, would be more acceptable to this difficult god. At least, that is what they decided.

The fire was lit and they all started dancing around it like men and women possessed. Soon they were in a trance and doing strange things. Some of them were crawling around on all fours, barking like dogs and chewing weeds that were growing out of the ground. Some were frothing at the mouth. Others lay on their backs in the mud and wallowed like pigs.

Strange shrieks rent the still night air. Then came the time for the offering.

Todd was already preparing to meet his Maker as he knew that he was in the hands of mad demons. And what a day to die! The same day that he had ridden the wave of his life.

They threw more dry branches on to the flames, which rose high in the darkness. In the light of the fire Todd could see the surfboard being carried on the heads of several excited bearers. Then it was thrown into the raging inferno. That wonderful board on which he had ridden the best wave of his life only a few hours earlier and which he had intended to keep forever. Todd knew that he would be next and was looking round for a way of escape but there wasn't any; wherever he looked the spears were pointed at him.

More dance and trance took place and at one time they were all jigging around him and touching him with the ends of their dirty fingers. And so it went on until the first light of the new day appeared. This seemed to put a damper on their spirits for black magic thrives only at night.

People started to drift away like the spirits of the night and, by the time it was fully light, Todd was being walked back to the hut. They had made their offering and had their ceremony and nothing like lightning had resulted so the god must have been satisfied.

Todd had served his purpose and was no longer of any use to them so a couple of them escorted him a few miles along a jungle track to the edge of their territory. He was handed over to the next tribe who were several degrees more civilised in that the men wore penis sheaths in the shape of g-strings and did not have bones through their noses.

Todd was given another escort and had to trudge through the sticky heat for another few miles until he reached a bamboo footbridge that crossed a wide, muddy river. The escort left him and he crossed the rickety bridge on his own. There was a track that ran along the meandering river so he followed it in the direction of the sea. Half an hour later he reached the inlet where his junk lay at anchor.

Kurt was more than relieved to see him back. When he had not returned after the storm, the German had wanted to report him missing to the authorities but in this part of the world that was easier said than done.

Todd decided not to reveal any details about what had happened. He did not want to relive it and no one would believe him anyway. He merely said that he had lost his board and then got lost himself and had to hitch hike back.

That night, when the two surfers were sitting on the afterdeck of the junk sharing a spliff, Kurt asked him, "Did you get any good waves out there?"

"The best wave of my life."

"I suppose you want to go out there again?"

"No. I no longer have a surfboard anyway."

"So there was a price to pay?"

"Yes, like all good things in life there was a price to pay. And the greater the pleasure, the higher the price."

CHAPTER SEVEN

GLORIA THE GROUPIE

If some people are born to be singers and others to be dancers then, as sure as birds can fly, Gloria was born to be a surf groupie. Her fascination with surfers and her insatiable desire to get to know them more intimately - especially if they were in the Top 44 - began when she was still at grammar school. With her pocket money she managed to buy every surf magazine that came out. The walls of her bedroom were covered with posters and photos from the magazines depicting whatever pro surfers were currently flavour of the month. While Heaven for some old men is sitting at Lords on a sunny afternoon watching England beat Australia, Heaven for Gloria would be to lie in the arms of the World Surfing Champion and let nature take its course.

When she left school she started to hang around the beach and surfers' bars but, apart from the occasional cheery "hello", the pro surfers with whom she was infatuated hardly noticed her. After all, on a scale of ten, Gloria, with a large bottom and a face that was terribly average, would score only a 4 or a 5. So, in order to be noticed, she decided to work at the surfers' bar where they all drank in the evenings. If she could take their drinks orders, they would have to talk to her. And who knows where that might lead to?

The only problem was that the owner of the bar didn't want any more staff as his wage bill was already high enough. That didn't deter Gloria; she just turned up at 10 p.m. every night anyway, picked up a tray and started walking around and taking orders all night. And she did get to talk to the surfers, some of whom, in a bit of an alcoholic haze after a night's drinking, would have raised her score to 6 or 7 out of 10. Things were looking up.

The manager of the bar was delighted; he had an extra waitress at no extra wage cost. Gloria was happy to rush round the tables all night and even help with the hosing down of the bar afterwards for no greater reward than the chance to get to know the customers. "Even slaves are more expensive than that," mused the happy manager. "They have to be fed and housed."

When Gloria handed the drinks to the surfers she usually ran her hand down their arm or over their hip as an added extra. And the boys returned the compliment. They soon began to expect it - not just from her but from the other waitresses as well. Unfortunately, the other waitresses were not so obliging and many a drunken surfer received a slap across the face when he stroked the breast of another waitress, mistaking her for Gloria.

Soon they were starting to take her to their parties afterwards and one thing was leading to another. But there were clouds on the horizon - usually in the form of other girls who were at least 8 or 9 out of 10. Gloria did not have many friends among her own sex as she was scared of the competition.

However, she never minded Fiona, her long time friend from school days. From Gloria's point of view Fiona had two advantages. Firstly, although reasonably good looking, she did not seem to be sexually attractive to men. But, more importantly, Fiona did not show any interest in surfers whom she regarded as being fairly juvenile and having one track minds. Always talking about the bloody waves! A subject in which Fiona did not have the slightest interest. Thus she was no threat to Gloria who was busy "getting to know" more and more surfers - both in the biblical sense and otherwise.

The problem was that the surfers who finished up with Gloria at the end of the night were not really the well-known names who appeared in the surf magazines. However, Gloria was taking it one step at a time and at least some of these surfers knew and even surfed with some of the Top 44 and so she could use them as a stepping stone to greater things.

She spent so much time following the circuit around that a couple of surf magazines got her to write articles for them on the different contests. They even paid her £30 for each article. Far cheaper than sending an editor out to California or Hawaii.

This gave her the power of the pen and the surfers, including some in the Top 44, began to be nicer to her and take her a bit more seriously. Instead of calling her "the town bike whom everyone has ridden" they now referred to her as "that chick from the surf magazine" and then, after she had written a complimentary piece on them, "that *cute* chick from the surf magazine". During her interviews with pros one of the questions that she always asked was whether they preferred long hair or short hair on a girl. After analysing their answers and finding that 70% preferred long hair, Gloria decided to grow her hair to below her shoulders. Things were looking up.

She spent her first night with a member of the Top 44 after the Hossegor contest although, to be honest, when he woke up with a hangover the next morning and found her crawling all over him in bed, he had to ask her who she was as he had no recollection of ever having seen her before.

Nevertheless, she was able to put a tick beside his name on her list of the Top 44 and she began to drop his name every few sentences. One thing led to another and two weeks later she managed to score another trophy. This one was a real catch as his ranking was Number 27 whereas the first one had been ranked at only Number 39. It was like climbing a tennis ladder. She was loving it and the guys were not averse to it either. At 4 or 5 on the looks scale, they were prepared to give her at least 7 for bedroom gymnastics.

Gloria was not choosy. So long as a guy was in the Top 44 that was all that counted. It did not matter whether it was a blond haired Californian or a black Brazilian, a clean cut city slicker from Sydney or a smelly, unshaven brute from the bush who beat her around a bit. At least it was another one to tick off on her list and another name to drop to her friends.

The highest one she scored on the rankings list was Number 8. Above that it was difficult as they were the more seasoned pros who had been doing the circuit for years and had come across her type so often in the past that they were now bored with them. Anyway, four of these Top 8 were happily married and the others found her a complete pest.

The one she was really after was Number One. But so was every other girl in the surfing world. In her dreams he always appeared as a handsome hunk of pure manhood who could surf like no one else on earth. She waited down at the beach for hours just to watch him surf, she tried to interview him for the magazine but without success, and she contrived to be at the same place as him whenever she could. She even did a night time raid on his clothes line and made off with his underpants. But that was as close as she ever got. However, as a consolation prize she scored another night with Number 8. And so a further tick appeared beside his name on her list.

She followed the circuit to Hawaii and, at her own expense, rented a large house overlooking Sunset Beach. She let some of the surfers stay there free of charge - including three from the Top 44. This had the added advantage of bringing others into her parlour as their mates (others in the Top 44) would come round to go for a surf or just to hang loose. But Number One remained elusive. He didn't even look up when, wearing only a g-string round her fat bottom, she brushed past him on the beach, the side of her naked hips rubbing against his.

She then decided that the surest way to get to know him would be for their cars to crash into each other. Then he would have to talk to her.

She stalked him for a couple of mornings and got to know his routine. It seemed that he drove down to the beach for an early morning surf and then home again about eleven. After that he would drive to the shopping centre.

The next day she put on a see-through top and the briefest pair of shorts she could find. She even polished the silver ring that she had through her navel. In short, she was dressed for the accident and so, looking more like a porn star than a motorist, she set out on her mission.

She waited by the side of the road until she saw the familiar white Ford hatchback come out of the driveway of his house. She quickly turned into a side road and then did a U-turn so as to be in position at the crossroads for a crash. Just a small one. She didn't want anyone to be hurt but there would have to be enough panel damage to both cars to warrant the exchange of names, addresses, telephone numbers, registration plates and insurance details. So much, in fact, that they would probably have to go into the nearby coffee shop to write it all down. And over a warm cup of coffee who knows what might happen? It was certainly worth a try.

She could see the car approaching so she went across the intersection quite fast and hit it on the front driver's side. There was a loud bang. Slightly shaken, she pulled up at the side of the road and so did the other driver. After checking her coiffure in the mirror, she got out. Now was her big moment.

She looked out for Number One but he was nowhere to be seen. The driver was a very large and very angry Hawaiian with tattoos all over his arms and belly. He had a long knife hanging from the belt of his denim shorts. "What the hell do you think you're dooin', you stoopid bitch? Greg loans me his car and you smash into me. Greg will be very angry. He my good friend. When I tell him that stoopid woman driver bang into me, he won't be happy."

"Then perhaps we should go back to his house and sort it out?"

"No, he asleep after surf. You give me details and then you hear from Greg's insurance company. Understand?"

"Yes," she muttered as she stared at the damage to both cars.

Later that evening she received a phone call from England. It was Fiona who said that she had some leave due and was flying out to Hawaii for a couple of weeks. Gloria invited her to stay. "It's such fun here. The Top 44 are always popping in and out," she boasted. Fiona wondered at the *double entendre*.

When Fiona arrived the house was so full of Gloria's surfing friends that the only room left was a little wooden hut in the garden. It stood on some short, thick posts and there were three wooden steps leading up to the door. Underneath the floor boards were some neatly stacked malibus. Inside the hut was a double bed with a carved wooden bedhead and a patchwork quilt, a table and a wash basin. Fiona was delighted with it - not least because it was away from the main house and all the surf talk that she found so trivial and meaningless.

That night Gloria took her out to a restaurant. "It's where all the top surfers go," she repeated a dozen times.

Inside Pancho's Spanish style restaurant all was noise and laughter, suntanned faces and peroxided hair, surf chatter and admiring groupies. Gloria was in her element as she exchanged greetings with all the surfers while studiously ignoring their wives and girl-friends. "Six of the Top Ten are in here to-night," she panted breathlessly when she returned to the table after her first circuit of the restaurant. She was positively beaming with delight.

"Well, I wouldn't know one surfer from another," said Fiona as she tucked in to her pineapple steak.

"I know almost all of them." said Gloria. "Some of them I know so well - even better than their mothers do."

"Oh, my God," thought Fiona. "How am I going to put up with this nonsense for two weeks?"

After the meal they sat on at the table and talked. Then Number 8 came over to say good-night. He said that he wanted to have an early night so as to get up and surf Sunset in the morning.

"Where are you staying?" asked Gloria.

"At the Hibiscus Lodge."

"Who with?"

"I'm on my own."

"Then I'll walk back with you." She turned to Fiona and explained how to get back to the house "because I probably won't be back until the morning".

"Fine," replied her friend. "I'll be on my way soon myself."

Fiona stayed on for a while as the music was mellow and anyway, it was all so new and exotic to one who had just stepped off the plane fresh from freezing England.

She started chatting to the young couple at the next table who told her that they were spending their honeymoon in Honolulu, having got married the previous week-end in San Francisco. "We got tired of all the tourist joints down at Waikiki," said the husband, "so we decided to drive up here for the evening. The whole atmosphere is different. This place is full of young people; there's so much energy. Waikiki is like one huge old people's home. It seems that the whole of retired America are staying there. And you should see all their unsightly bodies on the beach. Just like the elephant house at the zoo. But up here everyone seems fit and healthy. Where are you from?"

"England" And so it went on.

After about an hour Fiona accepted their invitation to go on to a late night bar for a nightcap. As they were going out the door the man plucked a couple of hibiscus out of a vase and placed one behind the left ear of his new wife (to indicate that she was already taken) and one behind Fiona's right ear to show that she was "available". And it was in these high spirits that they walked to the Hula Bar.

The atmosphere inside was very different from where they had come; it was filled with locals and there did not seem to be any surfers or surfers' girlfriends. For a nightcap the newly married man treated them all to a glass of *kahlua* - the delicious Hawaiian liqueur that is made with a vanilla stick and tastes like rich coffee with a real kick to it.

When their glasses were empty the honeymoon couple said that they had better get going as they had to drive back along the Kamehameha Highway to their hotel near Diamond Head.

Fiona thanked them for the drink and their company and was about to follow them out when she noticed a well-built young man giving her the eye. He had blond, curly hair and a handsome and suntanned face. He smiled at her ever so slightly and she smiled back. "I see that you're wearing the flower behind your right ear," he said in a southern Californian accent as he came up to her. "You know the significance?"

"Yes, the gentleman told me when he put it there."

"I should have one too," he said, "but I don't like drawing attention to myself; I'm a bit shy."

"I'm not shy," she said, "but I don't know anyone here. I've only just arrived from England."

"Well, I'm Greg."

"Are you a local?"

"No, but I come to the North Shore at least once a year so I know it pretty well."

"Do you surf?"

"I try," said the World Surfing Champion.

They talked about a lot of things. In fact, the only thing they did not talk about was surfing. Greg couldn't believe his luck in finding probably the only girl on the whole of the North Shore who didn't know who he was and was not all over him like a rash for all the wrong reasons. If she smiled and talked to him it was because she liked him for what he was and not because he was Number One on the rankings list. He appreciated her friendly, open and easygoing manner. And she obviously knew a lot about a lot of things. He liked to learn by talking to other people and he asked her many questions about life in England.

They sat on and talked until the bar closed and then Greg walked her home. The half hour stroll through the warm, tropical night was both exotic and romantic. They brushed past big leafed banana trees and bushes of hibiscus and poinsettias. Fireflies buzzed in the night and always in the background was the roar of the most powerful waves on the planet.

"Sounds big out there, doesn't it?" said Fiona. " Just like the Victoria Falls that I saw when I was in Rhodesia. Did you know that the natives out there call them the 'Smoke That Thunders'?"

"That would be a good name for Sunset," laughed Greg as they turned into the narrow lane that led to where she was staying.

"Is this your house?" he whispered when they reached the gate.

"Yes, but all the lights are out. Everyone must be asleep so we'd better not go inside."

"Well, where are you going to sleep?"

"I'm in a hut out in the garden. Come and I'll show you." He held her warm hand as they walked through the gate. Then they paused under a jacaranda tree for a long and passionate kiss.

Number Eight had got up for the dawn session and Gloria had walked down to the beach with him and then gone home. She had a shower and made some coffee and rolls for everyone. She looked out the kitchen window towards the hut and saw that the door was closed. "Fiona must still be asleep," she thought.

It was a fresh, warm morning and she remembered that her friend had asked to be woken up early so as not to miss any of the sun. So Gloria put a cup of coffee and a buttered roll on a tray and carried it out to the hut. She walked up the steps and opened the door without knocking. And there in front of her eyes was her best friend in bed with the World Champion!

At first she was confused and felt like telling this man, whom she had always dreamed about, that he was in the wrong bed. That *her* bedroom was inside the house. But then the reality of the situation hit her - her best friend, who had arrived only the day before and did not know one surfer from another, scoring with apparently effortless ease the one man whom she and every other groupie on the planet had done everything humanly possible to get their hands on. Poor Gloria! She let out a piercing scream, dropped the tray and ran sobbing from the hut.

"Who is that?" asked a rather surprised Greg.

"My friend."

"Is that how she usually behaves?"

"No, she must be upset about something."

"What's her name?"

"Gloria."

"You mean Gloria the Groupie? The silly bitch who crashed into my car?"

"Yes, I guess it's the same one. Do you know her?"

"Not to speak to. But it seems I'm one of the few in the Top 44 who hasn't slept with her. Sometimes pro surfers are accused of not having much respect for girls but it's hard to have respect for someone like that. She's like a community hot water bottle that gets passed from bed to bed and everyone knows it."

"So you're in the Top 44? You didn't tell me that."

"Does it make any difference?"

"No, I'm more interested in what people are like underneath and so far I like what I've seen. If you're a good surfer, then that's a talent you've got but it doesn't affect a man's character. Or at least it shouldn't."

"That's what I like to hear. Listen, I have to go down to check the surf. What are you doing to-night? Would you like to meet me for dinner?"

"Where?"

"I know a nice, little French restaurant at Haliewa."

"Not Panchos?"

"No. Too many surfers. And too many groupies. They bore me. When I'm out in the water I like to surf but when I come in I want to do other things and talk about other subjects. Just like we did last night."

They met for dinner that night and the next one. In fact, the more they saw of each other, the more they liked. Things went so well that Fiona quit her job in England and started travelling the circuit with him. They became a couple and, exactly one year after they met, they got married in the little Norman church in Fiona's home village in Devon. Most of the Top 44 attended. One person who did not turn up, despite the presence of so many top surfers, was Gloria. It was more than she could bear and anyway she was seven months pregnant. She did not know who the father was but she was certain that the child would turn out to be a good surfer. After all, its father was someone in the Top 44 or, to be more precise, someone who was ranked between Number 8 and Number 44.

CHAPTER EIGHT

THE ISLAND OF KAINUI

When Dean and Barry arrived at Papeetee Airport they did not linger very long. Just one night in the big hotel where their Sydney travel agent had reserved a couple of rooms for them. Early the next day they took themselves down to the busy port to catch a motorised outrigger which would take them across the crystal clear waters of the South Pacific to the island of Kainui.

Not many people went to Kainui as it was well and truly off the tourist trail - hard to get to and not a hotel on the island. Dean, a short, stocky young man with brown, wavy hair, had heard about it from a mate who had been there and who claimed that it had some of the best waves he had ever ridden. Uncrowded except for a few locals. Thus it was that the two surfers from Sydney decided to check it out and, if it was not any good, they could always move on to a better known break like Huahine.

The boat trip took all day and the warm sun was starting to go down when they finally sailed through the break in the reef on the southern side of the island and entered the calm waters of the lagoon.

They pulled into the beach and unloaded their boards and other gear on to the sand. Some of the natives came out of their grass huts to greet them. Upon seeing the surfboards the Tahitians told them that the best waves broke over the reef on the other side of the island.

Out of the growing crowd on the beach appeared a tall, well-built lad of about seventeen who introduced himself as a surfer by name of Moana which, he proudly explained, meant "blue lagoon". Barry thought what a wonderful name it was for a surfer. Moana, a dark skinned Tahitian with long, black, fuzzy hair, was wearing only a green lava lava around his middle. With a big smile on his face he began telling them how good the waves were. He offered to take them to his place on the other side of the island from where they could look out to where the waves broke over the reef.

Moana and his friends picked up the bags and boards and the two travellers followed them along the narrow path of crushed coral that wound its way around the hill to the other side of the island.

They could hear the thunderous roar of the surf before they saw it and, when they came to the end of a small coconut plantation, they could see line upon line of perfectly formed barrels breaking over the coral. They now realised why their mate back in Sydney had crowed about it in the richest superlatives.

Moana explained that it would not be dark for another hour and they could leave their gear at his place and he would take them out to make their acquaintance with the wave. It was almost too good to be true.

They walked on past papaya and banana trees, laden with yellow fruit, and thatched huts enclosed in colourful gardens that were blooming with red hibiscus. Some of the islanders came running out of their huts to get a look at the newcomers. They all smiled and called out words of welcome. Dean and Barry were particularly taken with the young women whose hips and naked breasts swung so gracefully as they walked. "I think we're going to like this place," grinned Dean.

To save what little time remained before dark they travelled out to the reef by motorised outrigger. As soon as they jumped into the warm sea and stroked their way out through the incoming sets they could feel the power of the waves that were speeding over the reef. There were five other surfers in the line-up - including Moana's younger brother, Maui, who was fourteen, and a Frenchman, Jean-Luc, the seventeen year old son of the island's only doctor. Moana escorted them up to each surfer who shook hands with them and welcomed them to the wave.

This side of the island faced north and the swell that it picked up originated in depressions as far away as the distant Aleutian Islands off Alaska. The wave itself was a long, hollow left which the reef held up for an incredibly long time. The two Aussies were just starting to get the hang of it when the light began to fade and they paddled back to the outrigger.

When they were back on the beach Moana asked them if they had anywhere to stay to which Dean replied, "What do you suggest?"

Moana said that there were a couple of guest huts in his family's compound and, since they were presently unoccupied, they could stay there and eat with the family. "Sounds great," replied the two surfers.

Moana's mother was very large and motherly and made them welcome in the usual warm Tahitian manner. That night they ate a hearty meal of fish that Moana had caught earlier in the day. And all the fresh fruit and vegetables came from the family plantation behind their compound.

Over the next few days Dean and Barry became acquainted with the surf, the island and its people. Most of the time they surfed with Moana and Maui and their friend, Jean-Luc. It was all so exotic and different - the brightly coloured flowers, the tropical heat and the natural friendliness of the people which was light years away from what they were used to in the rat race of Sydney where Dean worked as a computer programmer and Barry was a bricklayer. It was, in fact, the first time in their lives that people treated them like kings.

Whenever they commented on their fine treatment they were told with a smile that it was nothing more than "Tahitian hospitality" and that, if ever Moana or Jean-Luc should go to Australia, then no doubt they too would be treated as honoured guests.

"For sure," said the Aussies.

The hospitality even extended to providing a couple of beautiful young maidens to sleep with them. Huia just happened to follow Dean out to his hut after dinner and proceeded to take off her *pareu* and get into bed with him as if it was the most natural thing in the world.

"Tahitians always try to please their guests," she told him. She certainly pleased Dean - both that night and every night.

When Barry reached his hut he found the lovely Hinemoa standing there in the moonlight wearing only a large red hibiscus behind her ear. She told him that she was a gift from the gods. He believed her and enjoyed the gift to the utmost.

Despite all the night time activity the two guests managed to find enough energy to surf during the day and they revelled in the seemingly endless feast of barrels that broke over the reef. Their tube riding improved enormously; not only were there no crowds to hog the waves like in Sydney but, with a tide change of no more than six inches, it was just barrel after barrel after barrel all day long. "You almost get tired of the bloody tubes - they get monotonous," remarked Barry when they were paddling back across the turquoise waters of the lagoon after a five hour tube riding session.

Besides surfing they also went fishing with Moana in his outrigger canoe as well as diving in the crystal clear waters of the lagoon where they could glide among the colourful reef fish.

Almost every night there was a party as Moana's family loved to sing and dance. Moana always played the guitar. Most nights Jean-Luc and some of their other friends would join them for a sing-song in the warm night air and the two newcomers soon fell in with the easy and natural rhythm of island life. It certainly wasn't difficult; in fact, nothing was difficult on the island.

On Bastille Day they took part in all the festivities - even the canoe paddling race in the lagoon. And then, as the sun went down on that festive day, there was a beachside ceremony to initiate young Maui into manhood. An old tattooist, the oldest man on the island, was present and he made an elaborate, traditional tattoo on the arm of the young man which, like giving the *toga virilis* to a boy in ancient Rome, marked the passage from boyhood to manhood. Dean and Barry were impressed. It was certainly more exciting than the old Western custom of giving someone the key to the door when they became twenty-one.

The overwhelming impression that they got of the island was that the natives, although not nearly as rich as Westerners, were a lot happier and certainly more hospitable and generous. It was a veritable paradise but even paradise can have its dark side as Dean discovered one afternoon when he was stung by a Portuguese man-of-war inside the lagoon as he was paddling back from the reef.

He was in real pain so Moana and Jean-Luc helped him back to the beach and then took him to Jean-Luc's father who gave him anti-histamine to prevent the wound from turning septic as well as pain killers. "How much do I owe you?" asked a grateful Dean.

"Nothing. You are a guest on our island. Tahitian hospitality."

As they all got to know each other better Dean and Barry told them what life was like in Australia - particularly the beach life that revolved around surfing at their home break of Manly. "It must be great," said Jean-Luc. "If I pass my exams I will ask my father if I can go there and see you."

"For sure," replied Dean. "But Sydney is a lot different from here. It's a big, mean, hard city."

"I would have to sell many pigs from our farm before I could afford to go all the way to Australia," declared Moana, "but, who knows, one day I will get there; I know I will. I've read so much about it in the surf magazines. The furthest I've ever been is Papeetee but the first place I want to go to across the ocean is Australia. I'll get there - even if I have to paddle all the way in my canoe."

"We'll wait for you at Sydney Heads in a pilot boat," laughed Barry.

Their original intention to move on to Huahine came to nought as the island of Kainui had everything that any surfer could ever want - wonderful waves by day and warm women by night. The only problem with each passing day was that it brought them one day closer to the end of their holiday.

On the night before they left Moana's mother turned on a huge feast to which almost the whole island came. They dug a huge pit in the ground and roasted a couple of the pigs from the family farm. They sang, they placed garlands of flowers around the surfers' necks and some of them even cried. "And to think that I'll be back in my bloody office on Monday tapping the buttons on a computer," moaned Dean.

"What about me? I'll be laying bricks in the hot sun. We're starting a new contract just beneath the Harbour Bridge."

"Let's not even talk about it. I don't want to ruin our last night on the island with that sort of crap."

The next morning, after exchanging addresses with Moana and Jean-Luc and some of their friends, they boarded the same motorised outrigger that had brought them to the island five weeks earlier for the day long trip back to Papeetee.

When they reached the capital of French Polynesia they could not believe how much noise and bustle there was. And all the people! They had not seen a car for more than a month or even another white face - apart from those of Jean-Luc and his parents. They were unnerved at first and nearly got run over by a lorry when they were crossing the road, having forgotten that the French drive on the right.

"How on earth are we going to handle Sydney?" Dean wondered out loud.

"Dunno, but we'll soon find out. We'll be there in less than twelve hours."

A couple of weeks after their return they received letters from Moana and Jean-Luc, giving all the rather mundane news of their island paradise but, now that they were back in the rut of working in the big, brash city, it all seemed so far away - almost another planet. Neither Dean nor Barry were good correspondents and they never got round to replying to the letters. At Christmas they received a greetings card from Moana's family and another one from Jean-Luc but, since they were both going away on surf trips up the coast, they couldn't organise themselves to reply.

Then, six months later, came a letter saying that not only had Jean-Luc passed his exams and was coming to Sydney but Moana was coming with him. "We are so looking forward to seeing you and surfing with you in Australia," they wrote with enthusiasm. "We would like to spend a week in Sydney and then a week on the Gold Coast before returning to our island. We will arrive at Sydney Airport on Saturday afternoon at three o'clock on the Air France flight."

But when they came through the customs barrier at Sydney Airport there was no one to meet them. Barry the bricklayer was doing some voluntary overtime and Dean wanted to watch the League match on television as Manly were in the Final.

Jean-Luc believed that there must have been a breakdown in communications. Perhaps they had not received the letter. So he telephoned Barry's house. There was no reply. He then rang Dean's number but, because he did not want to be disturbed during the match, he had switched it on to the answer phone. Jean-Luc left a message saying that he was ringing from a telephone box at the airport and therefore couldn't leave a return phone number but that he would ring back at six o'clock. Which he did but by then Dean had gone out to celebrate Manly's win at the pub with all his mates. After work Barry went straight to his girlfriend's place as they were going out to see a surf film.

By 7 p.m. the two Tahitians had been in Australia for four hours and all they had seen was the inside of the sterile terminal building at Sydney Airport. It was getting late and, being strangers in a foreign land, they did not feel like taking a taxi in the dark all the way to the North Shore to try to find out where Dean or Barry lived. So they used some of their scarce money to stay in a hotel and decided to try again the next day.

They eventually got through to Dean at two o'clock the following afternoon. "Oh yeah," he said.

"I got your letter. Look, I'm sorry I can't have you to stay because I'm sharing a flat with two others and it's too much hassle to have extra people. It's not like Tahiti, you know. This afternoon I have to clean my car and I'm working all the week so I won't be able to see you for a while. But give me a ring later in the week - about Friday - and we'll see if we can meet up. See ya!"

Jean-Luc could hardly believe his ears and, when he related the conversation to Moana, the tall Tahitian was incredulous. So incredulous that he insisted on making the next phone call to Barry himself. He was beginning to think that he was in Wonderland.

This time the phone was answered by Barry's mother who said that her son was out surfing. Moana explained who he was and, without expressing either interest or warmth, she said that she would pass the message on to Barry when he returned. Moana said that Barry and Dean had stayed at his house in Tahiti for five weeks and that he and Jean-Luc had just arrived in Sydney and were looking for somewhere to stay.

"Well, you can't stay here," she snapped. "Both my husband and I work all day and so does Barry. We're all very busy and we never have people to stay. Try a hotel; that's where most tourists stay. Good-bye." A stunned Moana was still holding the receiver to his ear when he heard the loud click as she slammed down the phone.

"Well, they did tell us that the city was a big, mean place," said Moana laconically. "I now know what they mean."

CHAPTER NINE

THE GREAT DEBATE

The presidency of the Oxford Union, the debating society of Oxford University, has many advantages, not the least of which is that it is often a stepping stone to Number Ten Downing Street or at least a seat in the Cabinet. Why any normal person would harbour such ambitions, in view of all the criticism, abuse, lies and scandal that the public like to hurl at their ministers, is hard to understand but the fact is that ambition drives people to do strange things.

However, for the new President of the Union, Wade Cummings, the main advantage was that he had the right to select the subjects for debate and to invite well-known guest speakers to join the students in arguing the issues. Thus had been invited retired statesmen, philosophers, scientists, landed dukes, authors, sportsmen and entertainers. Most of the subjects were of general interest but Wade decided to include one topic that was close to his own heart.

Having been brought up near the coast in North Devon, Wade had always been a keen surfer. He usually managed to arrange his holidays to include a winter fortnight in the Canaries and another three weeks in summer in Portugal where he rode the waves to his heart's content - away from the grind of his studies and the responsibilities of the Oxford

Union. Hence the subject for the current week's debate: *That this house believes that competition is unnatural and undesirable in surfing and snowboarding.*

On the night itself the hall was full; by including snowboarding he had touched a well of interest since many students spend their winter break in the Alps where they try their hands at different activities and usually finish up liking snowboarding the best. And, of course, there were plenty of surfers as well.

Having never had the slightest desire to enter a surf contest himself, Wade took the affirmative with a rather out-of-it snowboarder who turned up for the debate wearing a complete snowboarder's outfit. On the other side were the World Surfing Champion and old Sir Bumble Baskerville who had won the bronze medal in the hop, skip and jump at the 1932 Olympics and had been on the gravy train of the International Olympic Committee (I.O.C.) ever since. Sir Bumble fervently believed that competition and money were the most important factors in any sport and that the I.O.C. was nothing less than the Voice of God.

The first speaker for the Affirmative was the colourfully clad snowboarder who wasn't nearly as stupid as he looked.

"Ladies and gentlemen", he began, "snowboarding, like surfing, is not something that you compete at; it's something you do. And you try to do it to perfection and with style. In this very personal challenge - the man and the snow or the man and the wave - you are the best judge of what you can do and not the rotation judge and the amplitude judge and all the other judges.

Snowboarding is all about having fun, getting a buzz rather than a medal. When a snowboarder whizzes through the white powder, he gets a rush and feels as if he is floating through the air - which he is until he comes down with a bump. Then, like a surfer, he needs to do it again. So, up in the clouds he goes in order to come down yet again. This is the essence of snowboarding - not competition. It is a powerful and personal experience, consisting of only the man and the snow. To tack on an artificial competitive element for the benefit of a few sponsoring companies is, I submit, as unnatural and tasteless as it would be to have a smelly McDonalds restaurant within the cloistered confines of Oxford University. It also spoils the fun. The fun is in the doing, not in the winning. The competitive element is, at best, contrived and, at worst, destructive of the very soul of our two wonderful sports.

Competition requires organisation, sets of rules, points, fines, penalties, bans and many other things that are the very antithesis of freewheeling, loose activities like surfing and snowboarding. That is why competition is so undesirable as the elements it introduces are at odds with the whole reason why most people embrace these ever so satisfying and deeply personal sports.

The very lack of convention is what attracts freedom lovers and pleasure seekers to the waves in summer and the snow in winter but all this is being undermined by the growing emphasis on competition which is financed and promoted by a few companies whose only interest in our two fine sports is how they can manipulate them for their own financial benefit. Pleasures like surfing and snowboarding are too precious to be ruined by crass commercialisation under the guise of competition.

And so, with one last clarion call that it is better to take part than to win, I urge you to cast your votes for the motion." (Applause)

The next speaker was old Sir Bumble Baskerville. A little the worse for drink he staggered across the floor to the podium and began his spiel.

"Mister President, my lords, ladies and gentlemen. I have never heard such rubbish as what poured out of the mouth of the last speaker. It only proves that snowboarders have a lot of growing up to do before they can be invited to dine at the Olympic Table. If they wear silly clothes like my opponent is wearing to a debate at the Oxford Union, then what on earth would they wear to the Olympic Ball? To tell you the truth, when he first walked in to-night I thought he was the Abominable Snowman." (Loud laughter by Sir Bumble at his own joke).

"Now, if they were to behave like other Olympic sports and *follow the rules*, it would be a different matter as they'd soon realise the importance of sponsors and money. And where would any sport be without those important factors?

Snowboarders have already embarrassed the Olympics by their antics at the Winter Games."

(Voice from the audience: "I thought the Olympic Committee embarrassed itself by its fixation with money and power - just like the Mafia.")

Sir Bumble: "Who said that? Take his name and I'll make sure he's blacklisted for tickets to the Olympic Games for the rest of his natural life. Now, as I was saying, the Olympics are about rules, reputation, respectability, maturity, commercial viability and, most important of all, television ratings."

(Voice from the audience: "Not sport?")

Sir Bumble: "There would be no sport if it wasn't for the money. And the surest way of attracting money to a sport is by competition.

I submit that it's in the nature of man to want to see a winner, no matter what the endeavour. We have Oscars for films, the Booker prize for books, Nobel prizes, school prizes and medals for sport. Yes, every sport. So why should surfing and snowboarding think they're so different that they can get by without competition? They must move with the times for, if they don't, they'll be left behind and will become the poor relations of the sports world. Is this what they want?

Professionalism, sponsorship, prizes and competition are as natural to sport as bat and ball. It is only competition that can generate the kind of hype and excitement which is needed to attract the all important commercial sponsorships. Without sponsors a sport has no future.

It is all very well for the clown in the snowboard suit on the other side to pour ridicule on competition but the fact is that there are millions who take part in surfing and snowboarding throughout the world and it is only natural that talent should rise to the top. It does in every other field.

It is natural for man to strive to be the best in any endeavour and he should be rewarded with recognition, prizes and sponsorship. Therefore, I say that this idealistic but very foolish motion should be defeated on the grounds that competition is both natural and desirable in every sport - including surfing and snowboarding." (Polite applause)

The next speaker was Wade Cummings who, besides being President of the Union, was one of North Devon's keenest boardriders.

"Ladies and gentlemen, surfing is many things - a pleasure, a lifestyle, an attitude, a means of self-expression, a beautiful art form and not, as our opponents are seeking to establish, a competition to see who can please the judges the most.

At its most basic, surfing consists of three things: a man, a surfboard and a wave. Nothing else. That is how surfing began and that is how it remains in its purest form. Unfortunately, we live in an age of greed and the surfing companies decided that, from their point of view, there was one thing missing in surfing and that was competition and all the hype that surrounds it. But there was a problem because waveriding, by its very nature, is not geared to competition and producing a winner in the way that a running race is. So they had to invent an artificial contest format which depends heavily on the subjective opinions of judges. In order to win, it is more important to please the judges and give them what they want than to let your surfing develop in its own natural way.

The man who knows how to do the particular contest manoeuvres that the judges are looking for is the man who will win the heat. And the contest. And the World Title.

Never mind that some surfers, like Cheyne Horan, try to be imaginative and experiment with different types of boards and manoeuvres. Cheyne had to stop his experimentation with star fins because the judges didn't know how to deal with any development outside the narrow parameters of their judging criteria. Therefore, rather than continue to lose points and thereby threaten his earnings, Cheyne had to scrap it and go back to what the judges were familiar with. This is a shame as, for the truly imaginative, there are no limits to the manoeuvres that can be attempted on the waves unless, of course, you are in a contest and have to conform to the established format.

The person who wins the World Title is not necessarily the best surfer on the planet. Theoretically, all the W.C.T events in a particular year could be held in small waves - maybe under six feet and so you could finish up with a chap who becomes World Champion without having to ride anything over six feet. Who would you rather watch? Damien Hardman in a contest or Brock Little at Waimea?

You will no doubt hear from the other side about how competition provides a challenge. That's true but every wave provides a challenge. What greater challenge than a bigger and more scary wave than you've ever seen before? That's the true challenge of surfing - not to see if you can get more contest points than the next man. Kelly Slater has said that the biggest rush in surfing is being inside a tube and you don't have to enter a contest to do that.

One of the greatest pleasures of surfing is the camaraderie out in the waves. If you catch a good ride, your mates hoot and congratulate you. The opposite is the case in competitive surfing because you're always hoping that your opponent will fall off his board so that you'll get more points and, of course, more money. Is that conducive to mateship and good feeling in the line-up? Competition by its very nature is fierce and the more prize money there is, the more deadly the competition and the more bad feeling between competing surfers. I'll go even deeper into the pit of controversy and say that those who regard surfing as primarily a means of making money are not true surfers and should stay out of the water.

Surfing should be about enjoyment but when a pro surfer, whose income depends on his contest results, loses in a heat he becomes downhearted and depressed. On one occasion the losing surfer and his angry girlfriend even threw rocks at the judges, who had to stop the contest to shelter under the table! Is that what surfing should be about? Allowing the money factor to destroy the fun of the waves? When money is at stake in a professional sport it becomes deadly serious - like a business - and it ceases to be enjoyable. That is the case with all professional sports like football, golf, tennis and now even the hallowed game of rugby. Do we want surfing and snowboarding to be the same? Surfing should be a passion and a pleasure - like making love. But we don't have lovemaking contests. That would be unnatural. So is a surfing contest.

Competition is an unnatural and undesirable intrusion into man's affair with the waves. I beg you to accept this point and cast your vote for the motion." (Applause)

As Wade sat down the World Champion walked across the stage to the podium to prolonged applause.

"Thank-you, ladies and gentlemen. I have listened to the powerful arguments of my opponents and, although persuasive, they are unfortunately not complete. Surfing is about an adrenalin rush and what more powerful buzz than to do a great manoeuvre *and* have the pleasure of beating your opponent? Competition encourages you to go the extra mile and pull off something exceptional. It's a thrill to do it and it's another thrill to win. A double thrill from one ride whereas the non-competitive surfer would not enjoy the second. In fact, he'd never know how good he is because he never competes against other surfers. At least the A.S.P. contest system provides a format where you can judge your standing by reference to your peers. And the judging system is not as limited or close minded as my opponent suggests. The really great manoeuvres in surfing are taken account of by the judging system.

If there was no competition, how would we ever know who was the best surfer?"

(Voice from the audience: "Watch Brock at Waimea!")

World Champion: "As Sir Bumble said, it's only human nature for a man to want to be the best. By gathering the best surfers of the world into a Grand Prix the standard of surfing is lifted. Through competition with each other all the time we are forced to draw out the best in us and make that extra effort which we probably wouldn't do if we were just playing around at our local beach which our opponents seem to suggest would be the ultimate goal in a non-competitive world.

Nor is it true to say that the competitive surfing world is riven by jealousy and bad feeling. We are mature enough to distinguish what goes on in the water from what goes on out of it. Of course we want to beat the other guy in the waves but we also like to have a beer with him in the evening. By travelling to the same contests the guys in the Top 44 are in each other's company an awful lot but we are more one big happy family than a warring tribe.

Contrary to what the President has said, the sponsoring companies actually do a great service to surfing by paying all the top surfers to travel round the world in search of waves. If they didn't put up the money we would not be able to do it. And many of them provide jobs for surfers after they quit the circuit. If this is being 'greedy' as alleged, then I'm all for greed.

Although I am obliged by my contract to take part in all the W.C.T contests I do not regard that as an imposition as contests are what I want to do anyway. For myself and other competitive surfers contests are both natural and desirable and for this reason I ask you to vote against the motion."
(Applause as he sits down)

And what was the result of the debate? Since you, good reader, have heard the arguments just the same as those who were present in the Hall I leave it to you to cast your own vote.

CHAPTER TEN

A TALE OF THE SIXTIES

The Bekkers had farmed in the Eastern Cape ever since 1818 when old Jacobus Bekker trekked with his herd of cattle all the way to this remote part of South Africa in order to get away from the British at the Cape who, by a series of interfering and oppressive laws, were making life unbearable for him and all the other Boers.

With the help of his black Xhosa farm workers the current Farmer Bekker raised both sheep and cattle on his fertile acres which extended right to the coast. The roar of the waves that were born in violent Antarctic storms could be heard from the whitewashed farmhouse which was more than a mile inland. Over the years the family had remained indifferent to the mighty ocean that lay on their doorstep as, like all true Boers, they were sons of the soil rather than the sea. In fact, the only time they ever put on their neck to knee woollen bathing costumes and went for a swim was in their swimming pool by the farmhouse and never in the ocean where the powerful waves frightened them.

The nearest settlement to their farm was the small fishing village of Jeffrey's Bay. Unlike urban areas like Soweto, which was a seething cauldron of crime and violence, this remote corner of South Africa was a little paradise on earth where everyone -

rich and poor, young and old, black and white - knew everyone else and life proceeded in an orderly, if mundane, manner. The men all had "short back and sides" haircuts and wore dark suits and white shirts to church on Sundays while the women wore plain dresses and big, wide brimmed hats to protect their delicate white faces from the burning African sun.

Visitors to Jeffrey's Bay were few and far between - sometimes a few day and week-end trippers from the city of Port Elizabeth which was fifty miles to the north-east but that was all. None of them had ever seen a Chinaman or an American or even a surfer. Which was why, when Astro arrived in the village towards the end of 1968, he created something of a sensation.

When he stepped off the old country bus that deposited him in the main (and only) street of the settlement, he was in bare feet with a brightly embroidered bag over his shoulder while under his arm he carried a ten foot long slab of yellow fibreglass that was flat on top but had a long, curled fin underneath. He was wearing a loose, shapeless *jellaba* that fell to his ankles and there were several pairs of brightly coloured beads around his neck. He had a brown moustache and beard and long, curly tresses that dropped below his shoulders.

From the bus stop the strange new arrival walked down to the beach, sat down on the sand and stared at the waves for twenty minutes. Then he pulled out a small plastic bag of what looked like plucked garden weed, rolled it into a cigarette paper and smoked it.

From their houses and fishing boats the eyes of the locals were upon him and they discussed among themselves whether he was a hippie or a trippie or an alien. After all, only black men got around without any shoes on, only women wore beads, gowns and hair down to their shoulders and nobody had ever smoked anything other than tobacco. As for the yellow, flattened out shark with the dorsal fin - well, perhaps that was his spaceship. A type of magic carpet on which he had flown down to earth from some other planet.

Then suddenly the strange looking man got up, took off his *jellaba* and stood naked in the sun for a few moments, looking out at the sea. A couple of the older ladies fell down in a swoon while the men muttered oaths and words like "Disgusting" and "Exhibitionist". The newcomer then rubbed some magic potion on to the fibreglass, put it under his arm and walked calmly into the ocean.

He threw himself on to the yellow plank and, using his arms, stroked his way out through the white, foamy sea. Then, wonder of wonders, he stood up on the thing and deftly walked across the ocean just like Christ did on the Sea of Galilee. Upon seeing this, some of the older ones immediately got out their bibles and started reading passages from the Old Testament as obviously a very divine moment was at hand.

He stayed out there for a couple of hours and sometimes disappeared into the breaking wave and then re-emerged further along. It was breathtaking to watch. At one stage he went through a school of dolphins that were probably just as surprised as the spectators on the shore.

When he finally paddled into the beach he seemed impervious to the watching eyes as he ran along the length of the beach in the natural state before putting a towel around his middle and wallking up to the general store. In his southern Californian accent he asked if there was anywhere he could stay as "this afternoon I reached my Nirvana. I've been going up and down this coast for weeks, looking for the perfect wave. To-day I found it and I want to get to know it better. I've got the bucks if you can find me somewhere to crash."

Unfortunately for Astro, this was a conservative and out-of-the-way place where, unlike America, the almighty dollar did not rule and people could not be bought. They were still in a state of shock - not only at the walk on the water but, more particularly, at his running up and down the beach naked. Why, even the most primitive native would have covered himself with a tiny triangular piece of material in the shape of a g-string. And now he was asking for some folk to have him inside their house! No way, José.

"There is nowhere to stay here," said the storekeeper. "We're only a small fishing community and we're not geared up for tourists."

"Tourists! Do I look like a tourist? I'm a 'traveller'. There is a world of difference between a 'tourist' and a 'traveller'."

"Sorry, we can't help you. If you like, I'll ring the taxi-truck to take you out of town."

"Don't bother. I'll find somewhere to live. Somewhere natural." He stormed out of the store and down to the beach where he picked up his surfboard and gear and started walking along the coast.

The land rose higher and higher from the shore until the cliffs were about twenty feet high. He walked for half a mile, checking out the land and the sea as he went. He rounded a rocky point and surveyed the brown cliffs which had been formed by thousands of years of waves breaking against them - waves that no one had ridden, at least not until to-day.

There was a narrow gap in the cliff and he went over to investigate. It was a cave that went in about twenty feet and had a sandy bottom. He could not believe his luck as he threw his things down on the soft floor of his new pad.

Astro was not the first man to inhabit the rocky hole in the cliffs for it had once been home to a clan of Strandlopers, which is the Afrikaans word for "beach dwellers". These were the brown-skinned, Stone Age race of Hottentots whose home was the beach where they lived off shellfish. The tide had washed away all trace of these simple, nomadic people and Astro was able to take over their former abode with "vacant possession" and surf this wonderful wave to his heart's content. As for the locals who had lived there for generations - well, they would just have to put up with this modern Strandloper. If they were unenlightened rednecks in buttoned up shirts, then that was their problem. The world was for everyone and he had certainly found his little spot. That mind bending wave that he had just discovered. He now knew how Columbus must have felt when he first saw the New World. All he wanted to do was to get back into the surf.

Astro had been riding waves for eight years at his home break of Malibu where he had always lived. He loved the ocean and indeed anything to do with nature. It was his way of reacting against the ugly concrete jungle that man had spread across the desert of southern California. Concrete was not the only thing that Astro rebelled against and the reason why he was in a cave on the South African coast instead of working in his father's stockbroking firm in Los Angeles was because of the little matter of the draft papers which he had received in the post. He had decided that, rather than risk his life in Vietnam - a country that he had hardly ever heard of and did not care two figs about - he would flee America (and the draft) and spend the next few years in sunny foreign climes.

He had begun his journey in Morocco where he lived in a commune in the desert just outside Marrakesh with a couple of dozen other draft dodgers and some rather easy girls who always wore lots of flowers - in their hair, behind their ears, around their neck - everywhere.

With loads of cheap hash and loose women it was not a bad existence but, after a while, he yearned for the waves and so he headed down to Agadir and Anchor Point where he was able to smoke the hash, enjoy the women *and* ride the waves.

In a further reaction against the strictures of Western society he began dressing like the Arabs by wearing a *jellaba* and colourful beads. Thus attired, he boarded the plane at Casablanca Airport and flew to Johannesburg.

The reason why Astro was able to spend these important years of his youth travelling the world, surfing its waves and wearing and doing exactly what he liked instead of trudging through the mosquito and snake infested jungle of Vietnam under military discipline and running the risk of being blown up by landmines at every turn was because he came from a rich family and, in the "great democracy" of the U.S.A., the rich have always had more rights than the poor. Only rich and well-connected people like Astro (and Clinton) could afford to dodge the draft. The poor had no option but to go to Vietnam and be maimed and killed.

Not that any of this ever bothered Astro; he was too busy enjoying himself to worry about others dying for their country while he had a free ride. And what a ride it was! Every day from the fast and hollow section at Boneyards to Supers and then on for about four hundred yards until the magic experience of riding through Impossibles and then on to Tubes. He did not always make it in one ride but, for perfection and power, it was unbeatable. He even shaved his board down to make tighter turns as this wave was in a class of its own. And the amazing thing was that he had it all to himself. Back in southern California it would have attracted a crowd every day. No way would he ever reveal it to another surfer and he knew that the locals wouldn't either. For them one long-haired Strandloper was enough and they would do anything to prevent him being joined by others of the same tribe.

They were still shocked at the way he surfed naked and accused him of being a mad sex fiend and an exhibitionist. The reason why he surfed in the raw was because it felt more natural. The sea is one of the greatest gifts of nature and Astro liked to get as close to it as possible and a pair of board shorts would have got in the way. He didn't deliberately try to annoy the locals for, in truth, he was indifferent to them. He lived in his own world and they lived in their's and, as Kipling wrote - "never the twain shall meet". He did not even worry when they held a public meeting to decide how they could get rid of him. All he knew was that he had one of the world's best waves all to himself and nothing else mattered.

The one who was the most determined to rid Jeffrey's Bay of its lone surfer was Farmer Bekker whose main complaint was that, after every shower of rain, Astro would wander over his fields and stop by piles of cow dung to look for gold top mushrooms. No one else had ever taken such an interest in cow dung (not even the vet). The nadir was reached early one morning when the big, brawny farmer spotted him crawling around on his hands and knees, moving from one pile of cow dung to another. He was even putting his head down to the ground like a cow to bite the tops of the mushrooms off their growing stems and gobble them down.

When Bekker approached him and asked him what he was doing, Astro stood up and started running around the field with his hands in the air calling out "I'm a magic mushroom. I'm a magic mushroom." Then he grabbed the crusty old Boer around the waist and led him in a waltz around the cow paddock.

However, the disgust at these strange antics was not shared by everyone and, in particular, the farmer's eighteen year old daughter, Lisa. She was a pretty young thing with lovely blonde hair and round, shapely breasts and was just at the age when she wanted to break out of the humdrum of rural life and do something exciting. And what could be more exciting than to become the first local girl to get to know the strange and mysterious surfer?

She had seen him on his board; it was an amazing sight and, to her keen eye, the image of him speeding down the face of a wave was godlike, gracious and beautiful. It was easy to see that he was well-built and well-hung but, in view of the almost universal animosity towards him, she knew she would have to be careful.

Towards nightfall she decided to take a walk along the coast in the direction of the cave where he was reputed to live. She knew the place well as she had been there several times for a picnic with her brothers and sisters.

As she rounded the point she could see him sitting cross-legged in front of a camp fire, cooking his evening meal. He was wearing a green sarong. As she walked past at the water's edge he gave her a wave that seemed to be as much a beckoning as a greeting. With a palpitating heart she changed direction and walked up the beach towards the warmth and light of the fire. In the half light she could see a big, blackened pot of water that was positioned above the flames and boiling madly. She asked him what he was cooking.

"Mussels," he replied with a smile. "I picked them off the rocks at low tide."

"Of course," she thought, "all Strandlopers live off shellfish."

He put an old towel around the handle and lifted the big, heavy pot off the flames. Then he carefully poured out the still sizzling water and left the mussels to cool.

"I live off these," he explained. "Mussels and salad on Monday, salad and mussels on Tuesday, mussels and salad on Wednesday....."

"Not much variety," suggested Lisa.

"No, but I'm not much of a cook," he replied.

"Neither am I," she confessed. "My mother supervises all the cooking. I'm more interested in sewing. I love clothes."

"I don't, but they're a necessary evil sometimes - like when you travel on a plane. I always wear a sarong or a *jellaba* as that way I don't feel so buttoned up. But I like your dress; it really suits you. Do you ever wear a flower behind your ear?"

"No."

"You should. The more colour the better."

"You like colours, don't you?" She was looking at all the coloured beads around his neck.

"Yes, it's good to be a little different and to put some colour back into our sad, grey, conformist world. Turquoise is my favourite colour. Probably because I love the ocean."

"Are there any colours that you don't like?"

"I'm not too keen on khaki and jungle green; they're too military. Have you ever been out of South Africa?"

"No, I've never even been to Cape Town."

"It's a big, bad world out there. You're lucky to live in a place like this. In the States everyone is trying to cheat and kill everyone else. The Federal Government is just one, huge criminal organisation that deprives people of their money by tax and of their lives in Vietnam. That's why I prefer to be here. I have a roof over my head, the best wave to ride, fresh seafood to eat and mushrooms every time it rains."

"Yes, my father told me about the mushrooms."

"Is he the farmer who is always smoking a pipe?"

"Yes."

"I don't think he likes me."

"It's just that you're a bit different."

"I hope so," he said before offering her a drink. "I've only got rainwater," he said, "it's all I ever drink. He stood up and walked up to a spot where water was trickling down the rocky face of the near vertical cliff and into a pot that he had set up to collect the drips. He scooped some of the cool, clear water into a couple of glasses and gave one to Lisa. Then he picked up his bag of dark green weed and rolled it into a Rizla paper. When it was lit he took a couple of drags and then passed it to Lisa.

"What is it?" she asked.

"Just smoke it. It'll make you feel laid back." She did as she was told and soon began to feel relaxed and at one with the natural world around her - the cave, the beach, the roaring sea and the fading light. Things started to seem a little different. For one thing, Astro seemed terribly powerful. And beautiful. It wasn't just his body but his gestures. To her small town mind they seemed distinctive, stylish, natural. So different from the rather awkward young men of the farming and fishing community. Plus he came from America. Lisa had always been fascinated by that big and amazing country. After all, it was the rock on which the whole Western world, including South Africa, rested.

She stayed for more than an hour and shared his meal with him. Before leaving, she promised to return in a day or two with some food that she would sneak out of the farmhouse kitchen.

She was as good as her word and another evening of eating and smoking ensued. This time she stayed a little longer and, when they had finished the meal and a couple of joints, Astro pulled out a mouth organ and began playing a tune. She was sitting close to him and could feel the warmth and strength of his body as she rested her soft head against the suntanned breast of the Strandloper. After another joint and a rambling discussion about the state of the universe they had their first kiss.

She crept around to the cave whenever she could without being detected by her strict and God fearing parents and it wasn't long before she was madly in love with the long-haired surfer. And the

141

forbidden nature of the fruit made it all the more alluring. She enjoyed the sensation of rubbing her fingers through his long, flowing hair; it was something that she had never been able to do to the local boys with their "short back and sides".

He for his part was fascinated by her seeming innocence, simplicity and natural behaviour. So different from some of the loud mouthed, gold digging chicks back in Malibu. Different too from the "flower children" he had been with in Marrakech who had names like Pixie, Raindance and Heavenly Spray. Lisa's face was pleasing even though she did not wear make-up.

She knew that her father would go ballistic if he ever found out as, after the mushroom incident, he always referred to Astro as "that animal who eats the cow dung". But the power of love has its own motion and things like hostile fathers have to be dealt with in due course.

It happened one evening when, instead of being back at the homestead by six o'clock as was his custom, Farmer Bekker had to tend a sick cow in the field nearest the beach. As he was riding his horse back along the clifftop he could see two people swimming in the sea. He knew that one of them would be the cave dweller but who on earth was the other? Surely another alien hadn't come to join him. He pulled his horse up behind a big baobab tree and, partly hidden by its wide trunk, he squinted the eyes of his weatherbeaten face to get a better look. The

142

two figures were now coming out of the water. They were both naked and he could see that one of them was a woman. They were holding hands as they ran up the beach. Oh no! Surely not! It can't be. But even in the fading light he could see the familiar profile of his eldest daughter.

Farmer Bekker did not call out and make a scene; that would come later. He merely climbed down from his horse and, remaining on the landward side of the thousand year old baobab tree, sat down on the grass and relit his pipe. He sat there for nearly an hour in silent contemplation before remounting his horse and riding home.

When he walked in the front door he went straight to the telephone on the wall and rang a couple of neighbouring farmers, telling them to come round immediately and to bring their *sjamboks* with them.

He then walked out on to the veranda and took his own *sjambok* down from its rusty hook on the wall and started swishing it through the air. It was made of rhinoceros hide and had been in the family for generations.

The *sjambok* was the symbol of authority. Every farmer had one. Originally it was used to beat recalcitrant natives in the days when police and courts were few and far between and the farmer's *sjambok* was the only thing that prevented order descending into chaos. But those days were over and it was many years since it had been used. In fact,

Farmer Bekker never thought it would be used again and certainly not on a white man's bottom. But, in view of what he had seen with his own eyes that very evening, the *sjambok* was the only answer.

Before they set off he and the other two farmers, all of them regular churchgoers and psalm singers, guzzled down some bottles of Castle beer in order to put some fire in their bellies for the coming operation.

Astro was just stubbing out the roach of his fifth joint for the night. Lisa had left for home half an hour ago. He was now in a mellow and natural world of his own as he sat in the warm night air and contemplated the swell. It seemed to be picking up. He lay down on the soft sand and stared up at the new moon. Stoned and contented, he soon dropped off to sleep.

It was in this state that the Boer commando found him. They crept up to the sleeping body that was clad in only a thin sarong. Suddenly Farmer Bekker let out a cry which was the signal for "Attack". Astro opened his eyes and saw the raised *sjamboks* about to come crashing down on him. As he lifted his forearms to protect his face he realised that the Third Boer War was about to begin.

The first *sjambok* to strike him was Bekker's. Although intended for his face, it stung him on his right arm. Others were coming down on his chest and legs. It continued for two full minutes until Farmer Bekker, now like a bull in a rage, ripped the sarong from Astro's body and started laughing. "You like showing it off, don't you, sonny? We'll see about that."

Frightened that he was going to be castrated on the spot, Astro rolled over on to his stomach and they applied the *sjambok* to that part of the anatomy with which it traditionally came in contact - the buttocks. This session lasted much longer and by the end of it Astro was unable to sit on his bottom.

When they had given him what they regarded as double the punishment they would ever give to a black man, they tucked their *sjamboks* into their belts and went away to have a celebratory drink. The last words that Astro heard them say were "Well, that's the last of the Strandloper. As soon as he recovers enough to walk as far as the bus stop, he'll be out of town on the first bus."

"Like hell I will," thought Astro. "This is my wave and I'm going to stick with it. And enjoy it."

He lay there on his stomach for many hours as it hurt him to move. However, the human body is a resilient piece of machinery and the next morning he managed to stand up and move around although it was another two days before he could sit down. A week later he was back in the ocean surfing his wave all the way from Boneyards to Impossibles and Tubes.

Lisa was forbidden to go to the cave ever again and for a few days a close watch was kept on her.

It was a week later when she let herself out of her bedroom window at three in the morning and, wearing only her nightdress, ran across the darkened fields and down the cliff to the cave.

She found Astro lying on the sandy floor in a deep sleep, his brightly coloured sarong tied loosely around his middle. He had smoked more than usual in an effort to dull the pain that still remained from his terrible beating.

In the darkness Lisa could not see the red marks on his skin. She stood there for a few moments staring at his body that was rising and falling in rhythm with his breathing. Then she knelt down, drew away the sarong and started running her hand up and down the inside of his leg.

It felt nice and Astro, dreaming that he was gliding through a bright and beautiful coral garden, could feel his manhood expanding. Then the awareness that someone else was in the cave broke through and he woke up with a start.

When he saw that it was the gentle and lovely Lisa and not some *sjambok* wielding farmer he calmed down and took her in his arms. He did not tell her what had happened but somehow she knew. They kissed each other wildly and then let their passions run free.

They hardly spoke and when they did it was only in whispers for both knew that danger lurked all around. Just before five o'clock she gave him a final kiss and then ran across the still dark fields and climbed in her bedroom window.

A few weeks later she realised that nature really had run its course and she was pregnant. It was what she wanted - to have a baby by the good looking and exotic American surfer. It was also the best way of getting back at her father for what he had done to her lover. She wondered if it would be a boy. Perhaps a surfer. In any event the child would be able to claim that its father was the first man to ride the great wave at Jeffrey's Bay.

When she told her parents one night after dinner they just sat there stunned. The matter was now so serious that it was beyond any ballistic response. Choices had to be made and hard choices too.

There was no way she could get rid of the baby as, although they were not above applying the *sjambok* across the backsides of troublesome farm workers and even more troublesome surfers, there was no way that they would murder a baby that was alive inside its mother's womb. That left either adoption or marriage. Lisa refused to consider the former while her parents could not even imagine the latter. What on earth would he wear to the altar for the marriage ceremony? His sarong or his *jellaba*? Or perhaps nothing at all? There would be no shoes but plenty of colourful beads. And how would he provide for a family? Where would they live? In the cave like wild animals?

Lisa relayed the conversation to Astro. He agreed with the general consensus against abortion. He thought that, to create a little life and then kill it, was against the laws of nature and anyway he had enough experience of the world to know that abortion is the all-time bad karma and he certainly didn't wish all that misery and unhappiness on a lovely girl like Lisa.

"We'll just have to let nature take its course," was all he could say. But he did wonder at the incredibly complicated situation that he now found himself in. Hell, he only came here to surf the wave and, just by being his natural self, everything had zoomed totally out of control. He even wondered if it would have been easier to have gone to Vietnam.

He decided to stay on and give Lisa moral support through her pregnancy but even that would be risky as she could still visit him only in the middle of the night. The problem was that she was more madly in love with him than ever.

He looked forward to her visits and hearing about how it was all coming along. She seemed to bloom as the months went by and, each time she arrived and they lit a candle, she appeared more contented than the time before.

Then one day, after he had not seen her for many nights, she came in the daylight. He was actually out surfing when he saw her familiar profile walking along the beach. Alarm bells immediately rang inside his head and he paddled into the beach.

148

He knew that there could be only two explanations as to why she was prepared to be seen approaching him in broad daylight. Either her parents had relented (hardly!) or something dreadful had happened. It was the latter as he soon discovered when she ran into his wet arms and started sobbing. She had suffered a miscarriage two days previously and was utterly devastated.

They went back to the cave to discuss it and both realised that the whole difficult experience had caused them to mature considerably. "Maybe it was for the best," he suggested. "Much as I enjoy the pleasure of making babies I don't think I'd be much good at looking after them."

"You never know until you try," she replied sadly.

After she had gone he took stock of the situation - from not only his own point of view but her's as well. What confused him the most was that, in this beautiful and tranquil rural setting with its wonderful wave and abundance of fresh fruit and fish, a person should be as natural and as happy as it is possible to be and yet it had been the scene of more difficulties, complications and heartache than he had ever known before. Free love was all very well but it certainly had its price. It reminded him of the words with which Dickens began A Tale Of Two Cities - "It was the best of times; it was the worst of times."

Astro knew that he was a wanderer and not a settler and that a young, impressionable girl like Lisa was probably attracted to him only because he was so different and exotic. He knew enough about her to realise that she could never adapt to his lifestyle and he could never join her world; he would not be allowed to for a start.

The next day he got up at the crack of dawn for what would be his last surf on his beloved wave. He savoured every second of it.

He wrote a letter to Lisa and left it under a stone in the cave. In it he told her that he was leaving for the good of them both. It was, on his part, an act of love for he was walking away from the very best wave that he had ever ridden and the likes of which he would probably never enjoy again - not even in Bali which was the next stop on his indefinite surfing safari.

In 1975, when the Vietnam War ended, Astro and all the other draft dodgers started to think about returning to America. However, in Astro's case, intention was not put into effect for another few years and it was not until 1979 that he decided to quit being a wandering surfer cum hippie. He was getting tired of lentils and rice and drinking only rain water and he started to yearn for a good, old T-bone steak. Thus it was that he exchanged his *jellaba* and beads for a suit and tie. It was time to end the "natural" phase of his life and begin the financial one. And Astro had to make up for lost time.

Back in the States he had no trouble finding a job. It was there waiting for him in his father's stockbroking firm. There were loads of good jobs for people like Astro who had preserved themselves all these years with a healthy, natural and easy lifestyle as they moved around the world in search of beauty and pleasure. It was only the poor chaps who returned from Vietnam with missing limbs, shattered confidence and serious psychological problems who couldn't find jobs or the wherewithal to provide for their families.

As Astro moved aggressively up the corporate ladder, buying and selling millions of dollars of stocks and bonds every day, he had very little time to think of his sojourn at Jeffrey's Bay or even to go surfing at Malibu.

However, his world turned full circle in 1998 when he had to fly to Johannesburg to negotiate a merger between one of his clients and a big gold producing company. The negotiations went faster than expected and Astro was left with a couple of days before he was due to fly back to Los Angeles. He decided to take a trip down Memory Lane so he booked a flight to Port Elizabeth and then took a Mercedes taxi down to Jeffrey's Bay.

The man who stepped out of the shining Mercedes was light years away from the long haired surfer who had arrived there by bus some thirty years earlier. He was now bald on top and had a horseshoe of neatly trimmed grey hair around the sides of his head. In his Armani jacket and brown sports trousers, with a black leather briefcase and mobile phone as accessories, he looked every bit the American stockbroker on holiday.

However, if Astro had changed beyond all recognition, so had the sleepy fishing hamlet of Jeffrey's Bay. The place was crawling with surfers - hundreds of them - and loud music from all the fast food outlets, neon signs flashing day and night and cars and motor-bikes roaring up and down the main street. All of Farmer Bekker's land was now covered with cheap looking holiday houses while noisy and dusty construction work seemed to be the order of the day.

He walked into the general store (which had miraculously survived this metamorphosis) and thought that he recognised the white bearded old man with a pipe in his mouth who was standing talking to the storekeeper. It was a much aged Farmer Bekker. Astro looked into the old man's eyes. They were no longer cruel but rather sad.

"I didn't think that you liked surfers," said Astro cuttingly as he looked the old Boer in the eye. "And yet I see that you've cashed in on the surfing boom by selling all your lovely acres for ugly housing development."

"Who are you anyway?"

"I'm the one who first rode this wave. You probably remember me from the night you attacked me with your *sjambok*."

"Ah yes, the Strandloper. Do you still drink rainwater?"

"Only with whisky."

Astro could see the old man looking him up and down. He seemed confused. "But......you're wearing clothes. Normal ones. And shoes. And you had a beard then."

"Yes, and now I don't and you do. Our roles are reversed. In the words of Shakespeare -

> 'All the world's a stage.
> And all the men and women merely players.
> They have their exits and their entrances;
> And one man in his time plays many parts'

CHAPTER ELEVEN

ESCAPE TO PARADISE

Neither fourteen year old Damien Grigg nor his younger brother, Jake, will ever forget the evening of 14th January, 1990. They had just finished a meal of roast chicken that had been cooked for them by the lady who was looking after them while their parents were away for a week's holiday in Greece. Suddenly there was a knock on the door. Damien answered it and found himself staring at a policeman and a policewoman. "May we come in?" asked the male cop.

"Yes," he replied as he stood back to let them through.

"Who is the next-of-kin of Graeme and Celia Grigg of this address?" asked the policeman.

"Well, I suppose I am," replied Damien. "I'm their elder son."

"I'm afraid we have some dreadful news. The plane on which they were travelling back from Greece has exploded over the Mediterranean. It is believed that a bomb was put on board by Islamic terrorists. There are no survivors."

A dead silence followed as all three of them - Damien, eight year old Jake and the lady who was looking after them - tried to come to terms with what they had heard. Poor little Jake was the first to break down.

The police stayed on for a few minutes and, as they were leaving, the constable put his big hand on Damien's shoulder and said, "You're now the head of the family. I'm sure you will look after your little brother just as your parents would expect you to."

The Griggs had always been an extremely close knit family and had lived in their rented house overlooking the sandy beach at Tynemouth since before Damien was born. In fact, this was the first time that the parents had ever gone away on their own. All four of them usually went on holiday together - generally to Cornwall but last year to Bali for three weeks where Damien surfed every day at Kuta Reef and thought that he was in Heaven. A heaven that, in only a few short months, had turned into the Hell of the terrible news that had been brought by the police.

Damien was extremely smart and had always been top of his class at the local grammar school. He enjoyed studying and learning about the world. The other big thing in his life was surfing and he was one of Tynemouth's keenest and most proficient wave riders. Sometimes, when the water was not too cold and the waves not too big, he would take his little brother down to the beach and show him the tricks of riding a surfboard. He enjoyed teaching him all the things that he had learned over the years - both in the surf and out of it. Jake, for his part, was ever so proud to have a big brother who was such a good surfer. They were probably the only brothers in Tynemouth who had never had an argument or even a cross word. Now, with the sudden death of their parents, they were going to need each other more than ever.

A few days after receiving the terrible news the lady who had been engaged to look after them had to leave to go back to Scotland and thereafter Damien, who was both streetwise and remarkably mature for his age, cooked the meals, cleaned the house and did his best to console and look after his younger brother. All went well until, exactly a month after that first terrible knock on the door, there was another.

This time it was the local social worker who had been sent round by the authorities to drag the two grieving orphans into the sinister and smothering net of government "care".

She was an ugly, overweight woman with a man's haircut who was regarded as an "expert" in "childcare" - even though she had never had any children and nor had her lesbian partner. When Damien opened the door to this awful looking dike he felt like slamming it again but, once a social worker gets a foot inside the door, that's the end of it.

Damien told her that they were coping all right and did not need any help or interference from strangers. He went to close the door but by now she had her big Doc Martin boot inside and was showing an official card and threatening to call the police and to get a court order the very next day that would place them both in a "care home".

Damien bowed to the inevitable and let her in. Once inside, she announced that she was there to carry out an investigation for the purpose of deciding what kind of "care" would be appropriate for each of the brothers.

"But we don't need any care," protested Damien. "I'm quite capable of looking after Jake. I'm the only one he's got left in the world."

"You are not of sufficient legal age to look after a child and he will have to be placed in "care". And so will you."

"In the same place?"

"Probably not," she replied coldly. "The age difference is too great and it is unlikely that we would find an institution that would be prepared to take both of you. But you would probably be allowed to see each other once a month."

Damien was so devastated that, in order to compose himself, he went out to the kitchen to attend to the T-bone steaks that he was cooking for dinner. The nosey bitch followed him.

"And who are those for?" she asked.

"For our dinner. One each," said Damien proudly.

"That's far too much cholestral to give to an eight year old. It's well over the government guidelines."

Like an investigating detective she pulled out her government issue note book and wrote down "Health of younger boy in danger due to excess of cholestral forced on him by older brother."

She then noticed a packet of Marlborough on the bench. "Do you smoke?" she snapped.

"Yes, my Mum used to let me," replied Damien defensively.

"Do you know that it is illegal to buy cigarettes at your age?"

"All my friends smoke; their parents don't mind."

Out came the notebook again. "Older brother smokes cigarettes. Younger brother at serious health risk from passive smoking and in grave moral danger from criminal activities of older brother."

It was then that her all seeing eye noticed the slight red mark on Jake's cheek. He had been trying to hide it from Damien all night and now this wretched woman had spotted it and was asking questions about it.

The problem was that, during the morning lesson, the teacher had told Jake off for getting his sums wrong. This, on top of the trauma of losing his parents, had been too much for an eight year old and he had burst into tears. Sequel: in the playground at lunchtime the class bully, who was twice as big and strong as anyone else, came up to Jake and accused him of being a sissy for crying in class. Jake told him to go away whereupon the big brute put his fist into

Jake's cheek and made him cry again. Hence the red mark.

However, he had got over it by the time he met Damien down at the beach after school where they spent an hour surfing. That had really perked him up. He loved being in the water even though he could not yet ride the big waves like his brother. Surfing was the best tonic to help them get over their great tragedy. When they had come out of the water Jake had felt ever so big and important on the beach when he stood talking to Damien and his friends who treated the grommet as one of their own. Having big friends like that more than made up for the bullying.

Jake remained silent when asked about the red mark and claimed that there was no mark there at all. The woman persisted and was questioning him with the same vigour and determination as a detective would interrogate a suspected murderer. He started to cry.

"Leave off him, will you," put in Damien. "It's no big deal whatever it is."

She swung around to Damien and accused him of beating up his younger brother.

"I did not," he shouted.

"No he didn't," blubbered Jake. But the social worker was convinced and that was that.

"Young boy at risk of physical abuse from older brother," she wrote. "A classic case of sibling bullying."

She looked in all the drawers and cupboards and then went upstairs to inspect the bedrooms. And it was there that she saw Damien's six foot six swallow tail leaning against the wall.

"Do you surf?" she asked sharply.

"Yes."

"How often?"

"Every day if there are waves."

"How do you find the time? Do you play truant from school?"

"No, I just have to make the time."

She had dealt with young surfers before in other families that she had broken up. She had always found them to be free thinking and unconventional types. And there is nothing that the "care" industry hates more than an unconventional one who doesn't fit the stereotypes that have been formulated by the social workers. There is nothing more dangerous to this sinister profession than a person who dares to think for himself and who might not be responsive to the social workers telling him how to live his life.

When they came back downstairs the social worker announced her interim findings. "When I finish my report it will go to the Director and he will decide which institutions to send you to. We should have a decision the day after to-morrow and I'll come back and tell you. In the meantime I forbid you to smoke any more cigarettes or to eat too much red meat."

"Will it be in Tynemouth?" asked Damien. "I don't want to go inland; I wouldn't be able to surf."

"You will go where we tell you to and you can't refuse. You are under the legal age for making such decisions. You will both become wards of court which means that you must do whatever the court tells you. You should be grateful that the Government is prepared to take such an interest in you. Not like India where orphans are just left to die in the gutter."

She said good-bye without smiling. In fact, she never smiled. Part of the uniform worn by social workers is a sad face as they go about their business of making bad situations worse and spreading misery wherever they go. And this was a really serious case: a young boy of eight who was "at risk" from an older brother who smoked cigarettes, beat him up and was a loose, free thinking surfer with hair down to his shoulders. An obvious case of rebelliousness. Future trouble.

After locking the door behind her, Damien went over to the sofa and put his arm round his little brother's shoulders. "Did you get the hang of what she was saying?" he asked gently. He could see that the freckle faced little grommet was struggling to keep back the tears. Jake tried to say something but couldn't.

"Don't worry, it's not going to happen," said Damien reassuringly. Jake stopped crying. He had complete faith in his older brother and believed everything he said.

Damien was thinking fast. No way was he going to let little Jake be put in a place of "care" where he would be sexually molested and abused by the sickos and perverts who run so many of these cold, loveless and abusive institutions. And as for himself being sent to some sterile, soulless place miles from the surf where he would be among total strangers. Never!

Surfing was the main thing he lived for. Shredding waves was one of the best ways of getting over the devastating blow that he had suffered. Every ride gave him a thrill. And paddling out was the most pleasant way to stay fit. Much better than jogging round the school gym. No one - not even the law - was going to take that away from him.

After his brother went to bed Damien counted all the money that was in the house. Almost six hundred pounds. He then rang the after hours number of the second hand furniture shop and made an appointment for their buyer to come round the following afternoon.

The next morning, after Jake had gone to school, Damien rang his headmaster and said that he was sick. The headmaster was not fazed and told him to stay in bed as long as was necessary. Damien was one of his star pupils and was the last one he would suspect of not telling the truth.

After he put down the receiver Damien donned a pair of brown sports trousers and a jacket and tie and caught the bus into Newcastle where he bought two one-way air tickets to Bali on Garuda Airlines. The plane was leaving from Heathrow the next day.

The furniture man arrived at 1 p.m. and Damien told him that they were moving house and wanted to sell everything. The man spent half an hour taking an inventory and eventually offered six and a half thousand pounds. Damien said that he wanted cash and the man, who knew that he could resell it all for at least double that amount, was only too ready to oblige. He went off to the bank and came back with both the money and an empty van to take the stuff away.

When Jake got home from school Damien gave him a suitcase and told him to pack what he could out of the few personal possessions that remained. For a moment Jake thought that he was being sent to the dreaded "care" institution and was very frightened - rather like the Jews on their way to Auschwitz. But Damien knelt down on the floor so that their eyes were level and said, "You must not tell anyone but we're setting off on an adventure. We're going to Bali. We have to leave to-night. Otherwise that horrible bitch will come and grab us and separate us for ever. In Bali we'll be able to surf every day. Remember how warm the water was when we were there last year?" Jake smiled. Not only would they be saved from the government child snatchers but they had a whole new adventure to look forward to on the most beautiful island on earth. What a time they would both have!

When it was dark they rang for a taxi that took them to the railway station with their two tightly packed suitcases, two surfboards and two skateboards. Besides each other this was all they had left in the world. It had all been such a rush and there was no time to say good-bye to any of their friends - which was probably just as well as someone might have let it slip in front of their parents who, out of a misguided sense of duty, might have alerted the authorities.

They slept on the train and arrived at Heathrow in good time for their flight. The girl on the check-in desk asked if they were travelling on their own to which Damien replied, "Yes, we're going out there to meet up with our parents." It was a white lie but he didn't want any trouble.

"Go through to the Departure Lounge," she smiled.

Once they were on the plane Damien had time for reflection but never for doubts. He knew that he was doing the right thing for both of them. Their young lives had been shattered enough by the plane crash. The last thing they needed was to be ensnared in the horrors of the government's "care" system. He knew that his parents would have approved of the daring escape; they had always stressed how important it was for the family to stick together.

He then thought of what lay ahead. The future was unknown and that made it all the more exciting. Damien had always been a radical surfer who loved taking risks on the waves. That was how he got his best rides. A yearning for challenge and adventure has always been part of youth's make-up but in the nanny states of the West the opportunities for adventure were now few and far between as anything that was remotely exciting had been banned or restricted by the government's over-protective safety brigade. Bali would be different.

When they arrived in the sticky heat of Ngurah Rai Airport in Bali they were tired and sweating but nevertheless exhilarated at what lay in front of them.

Damien knew the run of the place from the last time they were there and the sight of the graceful, bare breasted women carrying baskets on their heads, the smiling Balinese men in their colourful sarongs, the donkey carts, the rattling old bemos and the weird looking street dogs reminded him of those happy days when he was last there with his folks.

They rented a two bedroom house with a thatched roof near the beach at Legian and spent the first few days swimming and surfing in the warm sea and relaxing on the sand after their long and exhausting journey.

On their second evening they shared their table at a *warung* with a friendly German girl of about twenty-five to whom they related some of their story but not all of it. She spoke excellent English and said that, since arriving on the island, she wanted to surf but did not have the confidence to learn. Damien did a deal with her; he would teach her how to surf and, in return, she could teach German to both him and Jake. And so it was that their lovely thatched roof cottage became an erstwhile classroom.

Hilda spent a couple of hours a day teaching them German, Damien gave her surf lessons and he also spent time teaching Jake English grammar and spelling, arithmetic and geography. For a field trip they trekked up the slopes of Mount Agung, the great volcano in the middle of Bali where the gods are reputed to live.

Although they learned a lot from their new friend, she learned even more from them. She admired their spunk and courage in doing what they had done while their self-reliance, optimism, brotherly love and ability to get the most out of life - especially the waves - were no less admirable.

Their's was an unconventional education but it was also a lot of fun. There were no detentions, no bullying, no punishments for breaking petty school rules and no smell of sweaty trainers in the gym. Just warm weather, wonderful waves, plenty of interesting people to meet and gardens full of fresh fruit and tropical flowers. It was, thought Damien, the type of existence that any schoolboy surfer in the world would give his right arm for.

And back in England? When the busybody social worker realised that the birds had flown she was very angry. Not that she cared a fig about them or their welfare but she had opened a file on them and they were now part of the system and it would be a devil of a job to deal with what had happened as the system was not geared for prospective wards of court running off to Bali to surf. She put them on a Missing Children's List and then moved on to her next job which was to make a dawn raid on some sleeping children and snatch them away from their parents whom she deemed "unsuitable" for bringing up children.

After a couple of months Damien and Jake, suntanned, healthy and a lot more mature and worldwise than when they arrived, had to fly to Singapore for a couple of days as their two month visas had run out and could only be renewed by their leaving Indonesia and then returning again.

On the advice of another long term visitor to Bali, who had done the visa run to Singapore many times, Damien bought a quantity of artefacts, shells and clothes to take with them on the plane as part of their baggage allowance. He would sell them in Singapore to help pay for the trip.

On the night they arrived in Singapore they made their way to Thieves Market. It was dark and all the stalls were lit by candles. Everywhere was bustle, strange looking people and unusual food smells.

They were approached by an old Chinaman in striped pyjama pants and a grubby singlet who, seeing their bulging bags, asked if they wanted to do "business".

"Must see, must see," he said between spits that were hitting the ground in all directions.

Damien took the things out of the bag and, with the help of a hand held oil lamp, the old man inspected every part of every item, all the time calculating in his head what he could get for them at his stall in the market.

Then the bargaining started. It lasted for more than ten minutes. Every time the old man refused to budge Damien started to walk away as if to show his goods to another stallholder and then it would all take off again.

As the wily old trader handed over the money he told Damien that, next time he came to Singapore, he must come by and do some more "business" as he was the only stallholder in the Thieves Market who was not a thief. "Me Ali Baba; all the others are the thieves," he explained.

Damien, by now having some knowledge of the ways of the East and knowing that every penny was important if they were going to survive, counted the money and noticed that it was ten dollars short whereupon, after some argument, the only "honest" man in the market pulled out the missing ten dollar note and handed it over with considerable annoyance that he had been caught out by a mere stripling of a boy. He then carried the goods over to his stall, sat down in his wicker chair and lit a pipe of opium.

With the money he received Damien bought some electronic equipment which he took back to Bali and sold for a good price. Taking account of the air tickets and the cost of the various products, he finished up with a profit of more than two hundred pounds. Plus they could stay another two months in Bali.

This became the pattern of their lives and it wasn't long before the old Chinaman in Singapore began enquiring after bigger and more expensive quantities. Damien shipped a few crates from Bali to Singapore and a year later he shared a container with Jan, a Dutchman who was exporting beautiful teak furniture to Singapore and Europe.

Jan had to go to Holland for a few months to sell the stuff and he appointed Damien as his buing agent while he was away. A month later came a fax from Rotterdam for three more container loads; Damien arranged the order and sent it off, earning a decent commission for his efforts. Soon other commissions followed. The advantages of using Damien were that he was honest, he could now speak Indonesian and, unlike most Westerners, he was nearly always in Bali.

There was still plenty of time for surfing and the cost of living was cheap. The two Geordies had the opportunity of meeting an extremely cosmopolitan bunch of travellers who were forever passing through Bali like birds of passage and this broadened their outlook. They met others, not as young as themselves, of course, who were on the run from other things - nagging wives, creditors, the police.

Out of his growing income Damien engaged an American as a tutor for Jake and the two brothers lived an idyllic existence which lasted for many years.

Sometimes Damien had to travel to Singapore, Malaysia and Thailand on his selling trips and he would leave a much grown-up Jake to look after the Bali side of the business. Damien was forever on the lookout for new products; their enterprise expanded and provided them with more than enough income for their needs.

Jake became as proficient and radical a surfer as his brother and, when they got tired of surfing Kuta Reef, they would go to Uluwatu. When that got too crowded they would go to Bingan or Padang Padang. They surfed with guys from Australia and California and South Africa and got to know some of the best surfers in the world. Everyone was cool to them and Damien sometimes wondered whether the interfering social worker had not been a blessing in disguise.

CHAPTER TWELVE

ZAK THE ZEBRA

Zak was weird. At least that was the common view of all the bigwigs of the surf companies in Southern California. The problem was that Zak was easily the best surfer in California, if not the world, and yet he didn't have what all other top surfers find so necessary - a sponsor.

It wasn't that twenty-three year old Zak was ugly and would not have looked good in their expensive boardshorts. Quite the contrary. With his stylish blond hair, suntanned face, infectious smile and perfect white teeth he would have been a sponsor's delight - if only they could get their hands on him.

Another thing that set Zak apart from other surfers was that he had more than one string to his bow. He was as good an artist as he was a surfer. His studio, which overlooked the blue Pacific at Del Mar, was filled with his paintings that were worth at least fifteen thousand dollars each (and usually quite a bit more). Very much a "man for all seasons", Zak had worked hard at art school and was now reaping the rewards.

He painted landscapes of the sea and waves as well as still life scenes from the beach. He also liked to paint horses and he received many valuable commissions from the rich owners at the nearby Del

Mar race track to paint their winning racehorses. It was extremely profitable and, whatever it was that Zak needed in life, it certainly wasn't money from a sponsor which would put him under certain obligations that would interfere with his current freedom to surf and paint whenever he liked. When there were waves, he surfed; if it was flat, he painted. That was his life and that was how he wanted it.

His favourite surfing spot was the island of Todos Santos down in Mexico. He always kept a couple of his boards down there at the local cafe and, whenever there was a really worthwhile swell, Pedro, the owner of the cafe, would ring him at Del Mar with the news. Zak would then put on his black leather jacket, jump on his Harley Davidson and cruise down the San Diego Freeway to Mexico. Once across the border and away from the wretched Californian police, he would take off his helmet and travel as free as the birds and as fast as the roads would allow, his long blond curls flying in the breeze as he headed towards his beloved wave.

After a long and satisfying session riding one of the most thrilling and challenging waves on the planet, Zak would have a huge after-surf feast at the cafe and then say good-bye to Pedro and ride back to Del Mar the same night. Ah yes, the freedom to surf when and where he liked.

Another thing about Zak was his natural sense of style. It showed in his surfing - always graceful and fluid as he steered his board across the face of the waves and into tunnels of water. He had just as much style out of the water - his gestures, his grooming, his clothes. Things that would look gaudy and awkward on others seemed to fit Zak as if Nature itself had put them there. The colour co-ordination that he applied to his canvasses could also be seen in his attire. Sometimes he wore bright colours, sometimes pastels and other times skin tight leather pants and a white silk shirt. The only things he never wore were clothes which carried the logo of any surf company.

Nor had he ever entered any of their contests. He didn't need to as he was always featured in the surf magazines anyway because he was so photogenic - both in the waves and out of them.

Besides the awesome quality of his surfing he was also set apart in the waves by his accoutrements. Where all the other surfers wore black wetsuits and surfed on white boards, Zak surfed in a white wetsuit on a black board. That's why he was called "Zak the Zebra". If this wasn't putting two fingers up the entire surfing establishment, then nothing was. It also marked him out as the most distinctive man in the water and made him appear almost godlike as he danced across the waves and performed manoeuvres which nobody else could do.

In fact, Zak was an icon of California youth just as Jerry Garcia had been in the Sixties. He had dated some of Hollywood's top starlets and there was definitely a touch of glamour about him. That made him all the more valuable to the surf clothing companies which didn't see him as a surfer or even a person but solely as a means of increasing their sales by millions of dollars - if only they could sign him up. And the longer he stayed outside their net, the more valuable he became.

How they nagged him to enter contests! They always kept one wildcard place open until the morning of the event just in case he changed his mind. But he never did. And the more they pestered him and rang him up every week with higher and higher offers, the more determined he became to resist them.

The most obnoxious of the breed was Mr. Sneedy, the manager of the Greedy Surf Clothing Company. On several occasions he had barged into Zak's studio when he was in the middle of a painting and started reciting his piece like a parrot. One day Zak even had to call the police to have him removed.

Whenever Mr. Sneedy saw a white wetsuit on a black surfboard out in the waves he would paddle out to the line-up and have another go at pitching his wares. "Shove off, man," Zak would say. "All I want to do is surf and paint. I don't want to be a performing Ronald McDonald and have to jump every time a sponsor clicks his fingers. Can't you understand anything as simple as that.?"

Southern California is the very fulcrum of the aggressive, money grubbing surf industry and too much push one way tends to produce a reaction, which is just as extreme, the other way. And so it was with Zak. He absolutely refused to speak to Sneedy and the others and on one occasion at a surf party he even poured a jug of beer over Sneedy's bald head. The way that it flowed down his shiny knob was quite artistic and Zak wished he'd brought his paintbrushes.

But marketing men don't give up as easily as that and, when Sneedy's company put on their big contest at Huntington Beach, they were determined to use Zak's name in some way or another to boost their company's image.

Sneedy told his spunky, young secretary to go down to Zak's studio, select a painting of the waves that had been done by the Zebra and pay for it without revealing who the buyer was. It had to be an undercover operation as Sneedy knew that Zak would never knowingly sell a painting his way as he would suspect the motive for buying it. So the girl, with twenty-five thousand greenbacks tucked into her bag, cruised down the freeway, turned right at the Del Mar lights and drove slowly down the short street to the studio of California's Number One Pin-Up Boy.

The sight of the good looking Zak with his engaging smile sitting behind his easel made her realise just why her boss was so keen to link the company's name with this young man. However, she kept her nerve, smiled and asked if any paintings were for sale. Zak pointed to a couple on the wall, which he had painted on the North Shore of Oahu.

She spent several minutes looking at them before choosing the bigger one for the vibrancy, intensity and sheer power of the waves.

"How much is this one?" she asked politely.

"Twenty-two thousand."

She opened her bag and started counting the bundles of notes which she handed to Zak. She then asked him if he preferred surfing or painting.

"I enjoy them both in different ways as they both require creative imagination - what to do on the wave and what to do on the canvas. Unfortunately, the wave lasts only a few seconds whereas a painting can last for centuries. At the moment the paintings provide me with enough money to go surfing whenever there are waves." That, of course, was the problem - at least for the sponsor companies. This damned fellow had a private income and a mind of his own - unlike most of the other top surfers who have no talents apart from their surfing and so have to take whatever dosh that people like Sneedy are prepared to offer.

She said good-bye and walked out of the studio, the treasured canvas safely under her slender, suntanned arm.

Back at the office Sneedy was ecstatic. He claimed that it was cheap at the price as, by flaunting it round his surf contest at Huntington Beach the following week and promoting it as the first prize in the bikini contest, he would be able to do what he had always wanted - have the name of the hottest property in surfing associated with his grotty company - albeit by underhand means. And that is exactly what he did.

Zak was livid when he found out that the painting had been placed in a special display cabinet in front of the main stand and that his name as the artist had been plugged over the loud speaker at fifteen minute intervals throughout the contest. "Our company is proud to announce our close association with Zak the Zebra and we have one of his priceless paintings of the waves as first prize in the bikini contest."

"What are you going to do about it?" asked one of his friends.

"Nothing at the moment. Listen, why don't we drive up to Trestles and go for a surf? That's the best way to get over a problem."

They were in the water for four hours during which time word spread around San Clemente that Zak the Zebra was surfing at the local beach.

When he came out of the water he had to battle his way through more than a thousand people who had gathered on the sand to watch the legendary soul in the white wetsuit surfing on his black board. There were photographers, grommets, groupies, autograph hunters, old men, young lovers and even a few local drunks. And when Zak went surfing at Newport Beach the following week there were more than three thousand people there to watch him as well as three helicopters.

When Sneedy heard of this he made yet another telephone attempt to lure Zak into the arms of the Greedy Surf Clothing Company but Zak just put the receiver down in his ear.

Although Zak was called "the Zebra" he in fact had a memory like an elephant. Despite doing nothing at the time about Sneedy's crude attempt to jump on the bandwagon with the painting, Zak had neither forgiven nor forgotten and, when the Greedy Company held its next contest at Huntington, he decided to get even.

This particular contest was to be an all-time special for the Greedy Surf Clothing Company. Although he had not been able to snare Zak, Sneedy had used all his greasy contacts to secure the presence of none other than the President of the United States. Elections were looming and what better way for the President to lure the youth vote of California than by turning up at a surf contest and pretending that he was interested in surfing?

The day itself was warm with a cloudless, blue sky and the surf was really pumping. Record crowds turned up to sit on the stands or the beach or any other spot from where they could view the action. The prevailing sentiment was, "Yeah, it's great that so many good surfers are here and the President too but what a shame we won't have the pleasure of watching Zak the Zebra."

The President arrived at two o'clock in the midst of much hype and he immediately embarked upon what he did best - kissing babies and shaking as many hands as possible in order to get those all important votes. He took his place in the V.I.P. enclosure on the stand and Sneedy made sure that there were loads of photographers to take shots of him sitting next to the President.

A few minutes later the two Men's Finalists paddled out in the big waves that were breaking so cleanly. The President asked who they were and Sneedy told him.

Clearly disappointed, the President said, "Not Zak the Zebra?"

"No."

"Why not?"

"He's not here to-day."

This was a great disappointment to the President, for Sneedy was not the only one who was scheming an association with Zak. The main reason why the great man had come was to have his photo taken with Zak, the powerful new icon of California youth. That would translate into votes. Thousands of them. And now, robbed of his dream, he had to spend the next hour and a half sitting next to a sleazeball like Sneedy and listening to his inane conversation.

One of the finalists, the current World Champion, took a wave, ducked into a tube and scored a 9. It was a great spectacle but that was the last wave of the contest that anyone watched because a quarter of a mile along the beach could be seen a white wetsuit on a black board that was charging down the face of a perfectly formed wave like a man possessed.

"Look, it's Zak!"

"By God, it's him."

"Quick, let's go and watch him."

"Why hang around here looking at all this crap when we can watch the Zebra?"

Within a few minutes the stands had emptied and there was a human wave rolling along the beach to where Zak was surfing.

The President was quick to realise what was happening. His main quality was to sniff out votes - like a clever dog that always finds the bone. It was said that his nose could smell a vote at a thousand yards and he would rush to get it. There was no way he was going to hang around an empty stand looking at a couple of dots in the water when all the action was further along the beach. It seemed he would get his photo opportunity with Zak after all and then use it in his election campaign to suck in all those youth votes. Not many stars or celebrities had been able to avoid being photographed with this President and his ghastly wife. Zak was one of the few who had but now the President had spotted a way to change that.

With his nose for votes the President decided that, if the mob was going that way, then he must follow. "I think it's time to move on," he said to Sneedy with a smile. "Why don't you come with me and we'll go and watch Zak?"

To be fair to the President he was unaware of all the background and nuances of the situation and, despite what he had been told by Sneedy, he actually believed that Zak's performance was all part of the contest.

This was meant to be the greatest moment of Sneedy's life but it was fast turning into the worst. The contest was ruined by Zak's clever act of sabotage, all the spectators had left and now the President was asking him to accompany him along the beach to watch the bloody Zebra - in other words, to walk away from his own contest. And he could hardly refuse the President of the United States.

They walked along the sand to where Zak was surfing in his distinctive colours, the Secret Service men clearing the way as they went.

Sneedy and the President stood on the beach for half an hour, watching the awesome display of raw talent that was taking place in the waves. Then the President looked at his watch. He was getting anxious; he had to leave in twenty minutes and Zak was still out in the water.

He therefore announced to Sneedy that he would like to meet Zak and could he arrange it in the next ten minutes? Poor Sneedy. He told one of his minions to paddle out and convey the presidential message but Zak replied that he was enjoying the waves and didn't want to come in for another hour or so.

"But the President wants to meet you," exclaimed the horrified messenger.

"Look, all I want to do is surf. These waves are the best for weeks and I'm enjoying them. There is no greater buzz than riding a wave; meeting a president certainly doesn't match it. Let me have the freedom to surf when I want to. It's in the Declaration of Independence that every man is endowed by our Creator with the unalienable right to pursue one's happiness and at the moment I'm happy in the waves."

"But the President....."

"Go and quote him the Declaration of Independence. Thomas Jefferson's words. I'm tired of being used by other people for their own purposes. All I want to do is surf and paint."

When this news was conveyed to the President on the beach he maintained his cheesy smile and even broadened it as he turned to Sneedy and said, "Is there anywhere we can talk - privately? Just the two of us."

Sneedy was dumbfounded. What could it mean? Was he, Humphrey S. Sneedy of Huntington Beach, about to be offered an ambassadorship? Had his intelligence and charm so impressed the President during the course of the afternoon that the great man had decided to appoint him as American Ambassador to Costa Rica? Or even London? He had visions of him and his wife riding to Buckingham Palace in a shining gold coach to present his credentials to the Queen. And all the people cheering in the streets.

"Why, yes, sir," he replied. "We'll go up to the administration tent at the top of the beach." What a wonderful moment! To be appointed an ambassador right on his own beach. How the Queen will laugh when he tells her that little story!

Sneedy cleared the tent of the administrators and led the President of the United States inside where they both sat down on canvas chairs.

"Close the flap," said the President. Wow, this was getting really big time. Perhaps a seat in the Cabinet? A new position as Secretary of Sport? But when Sneedy turned round after closing the flap he saw one of the most fearsome sights he'd ever seen. The apparently permanent cheesy grin on the President's face had been replaced by one of the nastiest and most threatening looks that Sneedy had ever seen. The type of look you get when you cross a Mafia boss.

"I came here," said the President in a menacing tone, "to have my photo taken with Zak the Zebra and all I get is a slap in the face. What ya gonna do about it?"

"Do you want me to paddle out there and use physical force to drag him in in front of all the spectators and photographers?"

"It's too late for that. A photo with Zak is worth hundreds of thousands of youth votes in California and, thanks to your incompetent organisation, you can't even arrange something as simple as that. To get those votes that we missed to-day we're gonna have to spend millions of extra dollars on advertising." By now the President's angry face was only inches away from Sneedy's and he could smell garlic on the presidential breath. "Did you bring your chequebook?"

"Yes," replied a quivering Sneedy. "Your aides told me to."

"Then get it out and write me a cheque for two hundred thousand bucks. It'll go some way to repair the damage that you've caused to-day by failing to arrange what I came here for. And don't ever again try to play games with the President of the United States."

Poor Sneedy. He knew that, when faced with this sort of power, he had to comply. If he didn't, he would probably face a tax investigation. Or the D.E.A. would plant drugs on him and have him locked away in prison for ten or twenty years. He pulled out his chequebook and, with a trembling hand, signed a cheque for the said amount. "And who do I make it out to?" he asked. "Your party?"

"Just leave it blank. It's for us to worry about the details."

As soon as the President received the cheque he put it in his wallet and walked out of the tent. The cheesy, vote getting grin returned to his face as he walked to his car through a group of bronzed, bikini clad girls, patting them on their all but naked bottoms

184

as he went. "Isn't he gorgeous?" they kept saying. "He'll certainly get my vote. Such a nice man."

When Zak came out of the water an hour later the crowd thickened around him. No heat in the contest - not even the Final - had attracted such a large and enthusiastic crowd as this. As he made his way up the beach Zak caught sight of Sneedy. "Hi, Mister Sneedy," he called out in the cheekiest of tones. "Did you have a good contest? I hope you made lots of money."

Sneedy tried to say something but the words would not come. He was frothing at the mouth and had to be restrained by the contest bodyguards who told Zak to get the hell out of it as it seemed that their boss was in a killing mood.

"Gee, all I did was ask him how his contest went," replied Zak who then lost himself in the adulating crowd

CHAPTER THIRTEEN

UNIVERSITY OF THE WAVES

It was the year 2045. King William V, son of Charles and Diana, had been on the Throne for fifteen years. With global warming people were sunbathing on the banks of the Thames in December. Space suits were sold in all sports stores and there was so much traffic in the air that more people now died in plane and spaceship crashes than in car accidents. Britain had long since disentangled itself from the expensive and chaotic farce of the European Union and was once again master of its own destiny. As in Victorian times, it was again the richest country in the world - thanks to the massive oil discoveries in the sea around the Falkland Islands.

While the rest of the world had almost run out of the black gold the South Atlantic was producing a seemingly endless flow of oil and it was all in the territorial waters of the Falklands which was still a British colony. The result was a profit of hundreds of billions of pounds which, after providing the two thousand Falklanders with all their earthly needs, produced an enormous bonanza for Britannia herself.

Because life had become so easy for everyone, with electric carts dropping people off on their doorsteps, the authorities had become concerned at the deteriorating state of people's health.

Television and the tabloid press had virtually destroyed all powers of reasoning as no one knew any longer what was true and what was false.

Initially the government had been pleased to reduce everyone to the level of morons as that way they were easier to control but boredom soon set in and young hoons began to turn off their television sets and go out in the street where their favourite activity was to kill parking meter wardens.

Some neighbourhood associations, whose members had been terrorised by parking wardens over the years, even offered a bounty of a thousand pounds for every dead parking meter warden that was handed in. Just like catching rats. It was a profitable business as, after paying the bounty, they were able to sell the dead bodies on to a company that "defleshed' them and then sold them to physiotherapists and doctors as display skeletons for two thousand pounds each. A very good use for parking wardens! It was also a good way to get people off unemployment benefit - just go out and kill a few parking meter wardens each day and collect the bounty. Far easier than having to turn up at the dole office each week.

Although the authorities were happy to see people moving off benefits and on to the bounty, they were also alarmed because fewer parking wardens meant fewer parking tickets which meant fewer fines which meant less income for the greedy councils. And so they decided that something had to be done to give the youth of Britain something more constructive to do than wandering round the streets taking out sad faced parking wardens.

The result was yet another "new policy initiative" which took its theme from the old Roman adage "*Mens sana in corpore sano*" - A healthy mind in a healthy body. In short, education was to be wedded to sport - financed, of course, by the oil billions.

That is why eighteen year old Brook Townsend, who had just finished his A Levels, was so eager to be going to university to do a three year course in Economics and Foreign Languages (French and Spanish).

Brook was a keen surfer and he had chosen his university with care. One where he could surf as well as study. No, it wasn't Swansea. Nor was it Plymouth. Not even the University of Hawaii. Brook was one of four hundred students who had been accepted for the University of Albion which was a floating university on the cruise ship, S.S. Albion, a twenty thousand ton liner with several decks for tennis and running, two swimming pools, classrooms, a well stocked library, individual cabins for each student and highly qualified teachers to give the lectures.

All the students were surfers and the ship would sail round the world for a year, stopping off at the best surf spots on the planet,, before returning to Britain for the summer holidays. The next year it would follow a different route and so on. Thus were the students able to travel, experience foreign lands, study while at sea and, of course, surf. And then get a degree at the end of it! "Thank God for this new government initiative," thought Brook as he walked up the gangway with his surfboards under his arm, "and for all the dead parking meter wardens that brought it about."

At the beginning of October the ship pulled out of Southampton and half an hour later they were already starting their first classes in the various subjects. The lectures and study periods were fairly intense until they reached Tenerife in the Canary Islands where they stopped for a week's surfing.

While most of the students stayed on board, surfing by day and partying all night, Brook decided to take a ferry to the island of Lanzarote to stay with friends and surf the big stuff at La Santa. Plus, of course, he was able to practise his Spanish.

Soon it was time to get back to the floating university and so, with suntanned bodies and a better knowledge of Spanish, they waved good-bye to Tenerife and sailed down the coast of West Africa to Dakar in Senegal, a former French colony.

Here they found surf, beautiful French girls who were holidaying there and, of course, a French speaking population which enabled Brook and his fellow students to improve their French. Much of their exposure to the nuances and cadences of that beautiful language took place late at night in the form of pillow talk. And the waves held up for the whole week they were there.

Then it was back to classes as the air-conditioned ship headed through the tropics en route to Cape Town.

The Albion sailed into the harbour of the Mother City of South Africa early in the morning and Table Mountain was covered with a tablecloth of mist. It was summer in the Southern Hemisphere and already there was a lot of heat in the early morning sun.

Brook and the others spent the first day exploring the shops and docks of this extremely cosmopolitan city and much of the next week surfing its waves. He surfed both sides of the Cape Peninsula (the warm and the cold side) and fell in with the local surfing community, all of whom envied the surfing students their cruisy way of getting a degree.

They then sailed around the bottom of South Africa and up to Port Elizabeth, only an hour's drive from the legendary wave of Jeffrey's Bay which lived up to their expectations. They rode it at eight feet from Boneyards through Supers and down the point. It was the first time that Brook had got three tubes in one wave.

Christmas Day in the great port of Durban provided them with a feast of surf and they spent the next few days checking out the many breaks both north and south of the city.

After that they got down to some serious study as they sailed through the Mozambique Channel and up to the port of Mombasa in Kenya where they became acquainted with the people and way of life of East Africa and surfed the warm waves that roll in to the beautiful beach of Malindi. Then it was across the Indian Ocean to the Indonesian island of Sumatra where they dropped anchor for a few days not far from the small island of Nias. Here they were able to experience the power of a truly master wave and also to study village life as part of a field exercise in Economics.

The next port was Surabaya in Java from where some of the surfer students made their way to Grajagan but Brook and his mates chose to go to Bali instead where they did some serious surfing and partying.

The highlight of Brook's stay on the magical island was to surf Padang Padang. He rode down the winding track on his rented motor-bike with his board under his arm, passing neatly tilled fields dotted with palms and banana trees towards the roar of the waves which sounded like rolling thunder.

He parked his bike in the shade of a low thatch roof and made his way down the naturally formed steps to where one of the world's biggest and most grinding lefts was throwing itself over the coral reef. He felt a little apprehensive as he paddled out through the mountains of water. The sets were eight to ten feet and the roar and power of the ocean made it very clear that this was one of the most special surfing spots on the planet.

He wiped out a few times but, when he did get a barrel, it was a truly magic moment. The reef held the wave up - which was why Brook was able to duck into a clean, horseshoe shaped tube that lasted longer than any other he had ever ridden. When it finished he felt utterly drained but ever so stoked as well and he couldn't wait to get back out and have another go. Which he did.

From Java the ship made a leisurely voyage down to Perth; they were at sea for fifteen days during which exams were held at the end of the second term.

They berthed at Fremantle, the port of Perth, and surfed both the city beaches and the long left hander at Margaret River which was breaking at a very rideable eight feet. They also managed to watch a day's cricket at the W.A.C.A. ground where they saw England bowl Australia out for 146.

During their voyage around the southern shore of the Australian continent Brook spent most of his time catching up with his assignments and preparing notes from the textbooks for the exams which were fast approaching.

He was ready for a break when they sailed into Port Philip Bay on a summer's afternoon with the stylish city of Melbourne set out in front of them.

Brook and his chums, whose surfing was improving in tandem with their studies, spent the next few days riding such famous waves as Torquay and Bells as well as trying out the surf of the Mornington Peninsula.

Three more days of study while the ship sailed up the coast to Sydney, entering its magnificent harbour just as the sun was setting and casting its bright orange glow over the white sail like roofs of the Opera House. They berthed at the Overseas Terminal, in the shadow of the Harbour Bridge, and spent the next few days checking out Bondi, Coogee and Manly as well as that traditional home of Australian surfing, Narrabeen.

More exams were held as they sailed across the Tasman Sea to New Zealand. Although Auckland was the furthest point they would visit from England, they also found that it was the most familiar - a type of home away from home. Not for nothing was New Zealand known as the "Britain of the South" and Brook and most of the others on board had loads of relatives and friends to look up. Their colonial cousins were certainly envious of their curious but delightful method of study.

All that Brook wanted to do was to ride Raglan which had been featured on several surfing films starting with the original Endless Summer way back in the 1970s - in the time of his grandfather. As a result of the recent earthquake it now had an extra rocky point and the wave could be ridden for well over a mile. He rode it during a south-west swell and his legs got tired standing on the board for so long.

After New Zealand they had a long stretch of study as they crossed the Pacific to Papeetee, the capital of Tahiti, where they were able to improve their knowledge of the French language, French food, French wine and French women.

Brook went to the island of Huahine and rode the powerful right reef break at Fiti. He travelled out to the line-up in an outrigger canoe through water that was so clear that he could see the brightly coloured reef fish swimming around some thirty feet below. The sea was luke warm and he got barrelled all day as he surfed above the deep water channels where the waves were hollower.

Exams were on the horizon and the week spent at sea between Tahiti and Hawaii was a real swot session night and day. They didn't want to waste any of their valuable time in Hawaii slumped over their books.

Brook spent the first day riding the waves off Waikiki but the rest of the time was spent on the North Shore. The winter swells had died down but to ride Pipeline, Rocky Point and Sunset in any conditions was both an experience and a thrill.

Some of the surfer students who paddled out on the North Shore would never have dreamed of doing so at the start of the voyage but the steady improvement in their waveriding - thanks to stops at places like Jeffrey's Bay and Margaret River - had lifted their performance.

The trip across the Pacific to the Panama Canal was given over to the last of the lectures and assignments and preparations for the coming exams. There were only two more stops to look forward to before arriving at Southampton. These were the Dominican Republic and Puerto Rico. Both places provided Brook with an opportunity to refine his knowledge of Spanish and, whenever he was out of the waves, he spent as much time as possible conversing with the locals in a last minute effort to improve his fluency.

The day after the ship pulled out of Puerto Rico they began their exams. These stretched over the whole ten days that remained between the Caribbean and Southampton.

The papers were marked on the ship and Brook managed to gain an A and a B in French and Economics but only a C in Spanish.

"Don't worry," said his tutor, "we can fix that up in your second year."

"How?"

"We've just received our schedule for next year. When you come back in October we'll be sailing straight for South America. Down one coast and up the other. We're going to be three months in the area - Argentina, Chile, Peru, Ecuador and Colombia. There'll be plenty of opportunity for you to improve your Spanish."

"And my surfing," he replied.

CHAPTER FOURTEEN

SURF SHOP WITH A DIFFERENCE

When Mark Chivers finished his exams at Cambridge at the end of May he had four months of holidays to look forward to but with a bank account that was heavily in debit. He scraped together what he could, put his surfboard and other essentials into the back of his hatchback and took the night ferry to France. His intention was to work on the Mediterranean coast during the tourist season to improve both his finances and his French (which latter was pretty good anyway as it was one of the subjects he was reading at Cambridge). Then he would take the last month off for a surfing holiday in Portugal where the living was cheap, the waves were good and the natives friendly.

In order to save money he decided to take a middle of the night ferry, leaving Dover at 3 a.m. on a P and O vessel and arriving at Calais an hour and twenty minutes later. It was a smooth crossing and he had a cooked breakfast on board to fortify him for the four hour drive to Paris where he planned to stay a night with Sophie, a young lady whom he had met on the beach at Biarritz the previous summer.

Paris in the late spring was so seductive that he finished up staying three nights instead of one. He and Sophie visited the Louvre, climbed the stone steps inside the Arc de Triomphe, walked in the Bois de Boulogne and sat for hours on the terrace of a pavement cafe on the Boulevard Saint Michel just watching the world go by - students from the Sorbonne celebrating the end of the exams, tourists fossicking around the bookstalls, lovers holding hands and anxious looking office workers rushing hither and thither.

However, on the fourth morning it was time to say good-bye to the lovely Sophie and head down through the ancient heartland of France to the great cosmopolitan port of Marseilles.

Unfortunately, when he was on a roundabout near Aix-en-Provence, a big lorry sped on to the circle without any regard for what was already there and Mark had to slam on the brakes. In the process his surfboard shot forward and hit the dashboard. Result: a crushed nose (the board, not the surfer). The lorry roared off in the other direction and a badly shaken Mark restarted his car and proceeded on his way. "Damn," he said to himself, "I've managed to ding the board without even going in the water. First task when I reach the coast is to find a surf shop that has some resin and sandpaper." He always fixed his own boards but, in the rush of getting away, he had forgotten to pack his repair kit.

He arrived in Marsillles late at night and checked into a two star hotel near the Old Port that was run by an old man called Marcel. When he saw Mark carrying the broken surfboard through the door he looked at the ding and proceeded to tell the guest where he could find surf in that part of the Mediterranean. "Cassis very good," he kept saying. "Many surfers at Cassis."

The next morning Mark looked up the yellow pages and saw that there was a surf shop only a couple of blocks from where he was staying.

After a breakfast of orange juice, coffee and croissants he made his way to the Barbary Surf Shop to buy the necessary repair kit.

Although it stocked wax and resin and a few leg ropes and surfboards, it was really a clothes shop calling itself a surf shop. There were rows and rows of shorts and T-shirts and bikinis but only three surfboards. There was even a changing room for all the clothes customers.

The man behind the counter was an Arab who was about thirty and had a neatly clipped black moustache. He was wearing a fawn shirt and finely pressed black trousers. Mark asked for some resin and sandpaper "as I want to repair my surfboard".

"You can fix surfboards?" asked the man in surprise.

"Yes, it's not difficult once you know how."

"Many people bring their surfboards in here to fix but I send them away as I don't know how to do it."

"Do you surf?" asked Mark.

"No. Just sell surf gear in surf shop. No time to surf. Very busy shop - especially now that the tourist season is about to start."

At that moment a young boy walked in with a board that had a couple of dings in the rails. He asked for it to be repaired. Mohammed, the shopkeeper, was about to give his usual refusal when he was suddenly struck by a flash of inspiration. He asked Mark if he could fix it.

Mark picked up the board and had a look at it. "Yes," he replied. "These dings are not too deep; it shouldn't take me long."

"Very well," said Mohammed to the boy. "Leave it here and come back to-morrow. Two hundred francs."

Mark spent the morning in the room at the back of the shop fixing both his own board and the boy's. Two other customers brought in damaged boards and he repaired them as well.

He returned the next morning to mend one more board and then looked after the shop for a couple of hours while Mohammed went out. By the third day he had a job for the summer - repairing boards and serving in the shop.

As he got to know the owner better Mark came to realise just how little Mohammed knew about surfing. His expertise was in buying and selling; he was really a rag merchant with a few surfboards thrown in on the side.

There were other strange things that Mark noticed. When an attractive girl came in to try on a garment Mohammed appeared a little too enthusiastic with the tape measure on the inside leg and he seemed to look at spunky young girls with a rather awkward leer. And then there was his friend, Khalid, who used to drop in from time to time and stay for an hour or two, casting his beady eye over all the suntanned young things in their brief cutaway shorts and bikini tops. However, although observant, Mark was not judgemental and anyway, as the weeks went by the shop became busier and busier and he was so run off his feet serving the customers that he had less time to observe the two leering Arabs. Although not a groper himself he had to admit that some of the girls who came in to buy clothes were among the most beautiful he had ever laid eyes on.

However, not all of them were honest and on a few occasions he caught shoplifters. He was rather surprised when Mohammed always let them go without further ado. Mark wondered why his boss never called the police. Perhaps he had something to hide. However, as Mark reminded himself yet again, he was only an employee. And a busy one at that. Often he had to stay behind in the evenings to do the board repairs that he did not have time for during the day. Sunday was his only day off and he spent it surfing at Cassis if there were waves or soaking up the sun on the beach if there weren't.

As July turned into August, the traditional holiday month in France, the influx of gorgeous girls really began. Some of them even opened the door of the changing room to ask Mark what he thought of the bikini they were trying on. He always gave an honest answer and that was always positive. One reason for this was the very narrow door at the entrance to the shop. Whether Mohammed had deliberately made it so narrow he did not know but the happy result was that only people of slim or medium build could squeeze through. By keeping fat girls out it ensured that the subtly cut bikinis always looked superb on the body.

It happened one morning when Mark and Mohammed were frantically serving the customers and Khalid was looking on with his usual leer. The girl who came through the door was so drop dead gorgeous that Mark dropped the T-shirt he was holding and very nearly popped the buttons on his shorts as well. With her blonde hair, perfect classical features and flawless complexion she looked as if she had just stepped out of a fashion magazine.

Mark's eyes followed her as she walked over to the rack of bikinis where the price went in the opposite direction from the amount of material that constituted the garment; the briefer the bikini, the higher the price.

Mark could see her fossicking around at the higher price end of the rack. Eventually she chose a Brazilian creation and asked him if she could try it on. Despite his palpitating heart he managed to say "yes" and led her over to the changing room. She went inside and bolted the door.

Mark returned to the counter but kept his eye on the door for when the goddess would reappear.

Would she be standing there in the tiny bikini asking him his opinion or would she just walk out again as she had walked in, her see-through white, muslin top falling over her skin tight black shorts? Mohammed was still busy with the customers but Khalid had disappeared.

Mark waited and served another customer but he never took his eye off the door of the changing room. Nothing happened so he served another two customers. Still no sign of the classical beauty. What on earth was she doing? Taking advantage of the privacy of the changing room to roll a joint? Maybe even shooting up? Surely not. He started to look at his watch. Ten minutes became fifteen and fifteen became twenty.

He then asked Mohammed if he should knock on the door of the changing room "as the blonde girl has been in there for more than twenty minutes".

"No, no. She came out," replied Mohammed, "and walked out of the shop."

"That's not possible! I haven't taken my eye off the door since she went in."

"You should be serving the customers, not eyeing the girls. I tell you, I saw her come out and walk out of the shop."

Mark was sure that he was lying. He walked over to the changing room and knocked. The pressure of his knuckles caused the door to open slightly. It was no longer bolted. He looked inside; there was nobody there and no clothes of any kind. He tried the sash window. It was closed and would not move. It was then that he noticed something else about the room. Unlike the door of most changing rooms, which end a foot or two above the floor, this one came right down to the carpet so that, when it was closed, no one could see into the room at all.

Mark returned to the counter in a state of confusion. He rang up the wrong amounts for the next two customers. The first one he undercharged by mistake but the customer didn't correct him; the next one he overcharged and received such a loud bollocking that he was at last brought out of his daze.

As the afternoon proceeded he began to wonder if perhaps he had taken his eyes off the door. But he was pretty certain he hadn't.

At the end of the day he was handed his previous month's pay by Mohammed. When he counted it he found that it was two thousand francs too much. He pointed this out to Mohammed who replied that it was bad karma for the employer to take back money that had already been paid out. It was ten days before Khalid appeared again.

The long week-end of 15th August was the feast of the Assumption. It was also the busiest week-end of the year in the tourist areas - including the Barbary Surf Shop.

It was late in the afternoon and the shop was starting to fill up after the siesta and the beach. This time the blonde girl who came through the door was even more strikingly beautiful than the one whose

203

disappearance earlier in the month had caused Mark so much anxiety and doubt. She had long, blonde hair which seemed to shimmer in the late afternoon sun that was coming through the shop window. Mark just loved that sort of hair on a girl, believing that it accentuated her femininity.

As usual, the creepy Khalid gave her the once over with his wandering eyes as she made her way to the shorts section where she started to rummage through all the highly priced garments on the rack. She picked out a pair of shorts in earthy colours and asked Mark if she could try them on.

He was busy serving another customer so he pointed to the changing room and told her to go in. He never took his eyes off her as she walked across the wooden floor of the shop in the direction of the changing room. And he'd never seen hips swing so sensually. She was wearing high platform shoes which accentuated her long and shapely legs. Then the door closed.

The shop was full and there was a lot of noise as the customers talked and laughed while making their way along the clothes racks. All Mark wanted to see was that wonderful figure come prancing out of the changing room. He stood at the counter serving more customers but he never took his eye off the door of the changing room which, however, remained firmly closed.

After about quarter of an hour he was seized by panic and a sense of *déjà vu* so he rushed over to the changing room to bang on the door. It opened easily and there was nobody there. Nor any sign that it had recently been occupied.

In a sweat he ran outside and the first thing he noticed was that the sleazy Khalid was no longer standing by the door. Come to think of it, Mark had not seen him for some time. Not since the girl had walked into the changing room.

In the afternoon heat Mark ran around the block, looking at all the people and the vehicles in his search for the girl. But without success. He was in a quandary and didn't know what to do; hell, he was only a surf shop attendant and not Sherlock Holmes. So, after calming down a little, he returned to the surf shop. Mohammed saw that he was sweating profusely and asked him if he was all right. "That blonde girl. She went into the changing room and never came out. This time I'm certain," declared Mark.

"You are mistaken, my friend," replied Mohammed. "I saw her come out ten minutes ago and leave the shop. Now, calm down and get back to your duties. The shop closes in half an hour."

Mark's mind was so distracted that he was virtually on auto-pilot as he dealt with the remaining customers.

When closing time came and he went out to the room at the back to collect his bag he noticed a bundle of cash on the bench beside it. He counted it. Six thousand francs. His "keep quiet" money.

Instead of going back to where he was staying, Mark made his way to the Gendarmerie and demanded to see the Officier de Police Judiciairie. He told him what had happened - both to-day and earlier in the month - and declared that there was no way he was ever going to set foot again in what he alleged was "a pick-up point for the white slave trade disguised as a surf shop".

"It is a big problem," said the Officier, "and what you say fits the picture of what goes on. It is always blonde girls they want; the sheikhs in Arabia pay so much for blondes that it makes the whole exercise worthwhile for the middlemen."

"Last time Khalid was away for ten days," said Mark. "Enough time to drive her all the way to Arabia - drugged, no doubt, in the back of a closed van."

"Unfortunately, there is little we can do. The smugglers are so clever and it is like looking for a needle in a haystack."

"Why don't you set up a road block on the Italian border? Search every vehicle inside out."

"That would not necessarily find her. Arabia is not the only market for these blonde girls. Sometimes they are taken west into Spain and from there into Morocco. Others are sent by ship to North Africa. We can not search every ship in the harbour. And anyway, they probably have her bound and gagged in a false hold."

Mark was nearly out of his mind; he was also angry at what he considered was a lack of enthusiasm on the part of the Officier.

After leaving the Gendarmerie Mark lit a cigarette and wandered down to the Old Port. He wanted to spend some time on his own to think things out and also to have something to eat.

He found a restaurant that had an outdoor terrace which overlooked the quay. He sat down at a table and ordered a plate of mussels and some wine. Through the fading light he could see some fishermen who were trying to sell their catch of squid and eels on the concrete quay below. Behind them were all the fishing boats, some of which were turning on their night lights. Strolling along the quay in the salty air and trying to dodge the skateboarders were old men, bearded sailors and young lovers.

Mark took a sip of the wine that the waiter brought to the table. A good Bordeaux - not too heavy. He looked down again at all the people sauntering along the quay of this ancient port that had been a departure point for the Crusades. Apart from the skateboarders no one seemed to be moving very fast; it was that time of day when people no longer had to rush to appointments. Perhaps that was why he took special notice of the two men who seemed to be walking faster than anyone else; they seemed to be in a hurry to get somewhere. It was nearly dark but he was still able to recognise Khalid who was in close and anxious conversation with another Arab. As with the door of the changing room Mark never took his eyes off them but this time he was determined not to let the target out of his sight. He paid the waiter for the wine, cancelled the mussels and rose from his table to pursue them.

They were walking in the direction of the stone steps where some of the fishing boats were tied up. Like a sleuth Mark followed - but at a distance. He managed to stay out of sight - thanks to the diminishing light. He watched as they descended the ancient stone steps to the water and then climbed into a small dinghy with an outboard motor. He heard them start the engine and putt-putt their way through the maze of craft to a motor launch that was riding at anchor about a hundred yards from the quay. Mark could barely see it through the approaching darkness but was helped by the sound of the motor which came to a stop when it reached the vessel. He took its bearings and looked round for a telephone box.

There was one nearby so he rushed in, rang the gendarmerie and demanded to be put through to the Officier.

At first the cop was reluctant to do anything as the accusation against Khalid was circumstantial to say the least. He had merely been in the shop when the girl had allegedly disappeared. The Officier was not keen to ask the marine police to mount a raid - not least because he didn't get on with the marine chief. However, he was eventually brought round by the passion and urgency of Mark's pleadings, not to mention his description of the girl as "the most beautiful I've ever laid eyes on." The Officier put down the phone and immediately contacted the marine police at Fort Saint-Jean.

Mark waited by the stone steps as instructed. A few minutes later the rubber dinghy of the harbour police, with an almost silent motor, arrived alongside the steps and Mark was told to jump on board. As they glided through the now darkened water he really had to concentrate his eyes and his other senses on the target vessel.

Presently they were upon her and the harbour detectives, all wearing the clothes of ordinary seamen, scaled the suspect vessel like pirates. Mark, who had been told to stay in the rubber dinghy, heard some shouts and screams. What he could not see was Khalid reaching out to grab a Walther P 38 pistol. But he wasn't fast enough.

One of the cops shot him in the chest and he fell down on the oil stained deck in a screaming, bleeding heap. A few seconds later he died.

The police overcame the rest of the Arabs on board and then started a thorough search of the vessel. They even broke down doors and bulkheads with their axes and crowbars and that is how they found the object of the search. She was sitting on the deck of a small, dirty cabin that had been securely locked. She was still drowsy from the effects of the odourless gas which had overpowered her in the changing room and caused her to fall down unconscious on the floor before being spirited through the window by the man whose corpse was now attracting flies on the deck.

When she did not reply to their *"Bonsoirs"* the police tapped her lightly on her soft cheeks. Slowly she opened her eyes and stared vacantly into space. Even in this strange state the men of the harbour police couldn't help noticing how beautiful she was. One of them pulled a hip flask out of his pocket and gave her some brandy to drink. It had the desired effect and a few minutes later they helped her on to the main deck. Mark was summoned on board to make the required identification and, yes, he was able to confirm that this was the girl who had disappeared from the surf shop some three hours earlier.

The fresh night air had the effect of reviving her and she was soon able to stand unsteadily on her feet. A few minutes later they put her in a fishing net and lowered her into the rubber dinghy. She was taken to the quay with Mark while the police remained on board to keep watch on the crew who were all under arrest.

Mark accompanied her to the marine police station where she was given some hot coffee. When the Officier arrived and saw what had been achieved he was generous in his praise of Mark, whose presence of mind and amateur detective work had brought about such a satisfactory result. She tried to smile but there were too many tears in her eyes.

That night Ingrid was kept in hospital for observation but was discharged the next morning. That was not the only thing that happened that day. For one thing, it was the last day of the Barbary Surf Shop.

The police did not have enough evidence to arrest Mohammed; the only one who could have provided any evidence that he was an accomplice was Khalid and he was dead. However, when the law visited the surf shop at 10 a.m. they found that Mohammed was *sans papiers* (without proper papers) and he was arrested and deported to his home state in the Persian Gulf.

When Mark returned to the gendarmerie at midday Ingrid was there too and they left together. She was now fully recovered and insisted on buying lunch for the man to whom she owed her deliverance. They found a small seafood restaurant and took a seat near the window that overlooked the harbour.

Mark could see that she was still fairly frightened and shaken but, after a couple of bottles of wine, she began to loosen up. She explained how she was from Norway and still had three weeks of her holiday left but wanted to get out of Marseilles as soon as possible because of what had happened.

Mark, who couldn't take his eyes off her beautiful face and body, said that he too wanted to leave and drive to Portugal as he had always intended. After another bottle of Chardonnay it just sort of happened. There was a spare seat in the car and who better to fill it than the most beautiful girl he had ever seen? For her part it offered an attractive escape with the good looking surfer who had saved her from a fate worse than death - the same fate that was presently being suffered by the first girl who had disappeared and who was now being kept prisoner in a dungeon in Arabia where her sole function was to service the animal instincts of the fat, smelly sheikh who had bought her.

They left that evening on the long drive to Portugal where Mark rode the best waves of his life and also taught Ingrid how to stand up on a surfboard and ride it.

The sun shone continuously and every day and every night seemed better than the one before. Ingrid found that Mark, besides being handsome and a good surfer, was kind hearted and great fun to be with. And he soon discoverd that her inner qualities were just as fine as her outward appearance. Founded in the most unlikely of circumstances, their romance flourished and the following year, after his graduation, Mark flew to Oslo for the wedding ceremony. No knight in shining armour had ever won his fair maiden with greater gallantry.

CHAPTER FIFTEEN

TO RIDE A DISTANT WAVE

A Rhodesian surfer is almost as rare a species as the white rhino. Although former World Champion, Martin Potter, spent his childhood years growing up in that wonderful inland country in Central Africa, few other Rhodesians have ever graced the waves on a surfboard. Hamish Grant, who had been brought up on his father's cattle farm in eastern Rhodesia, was one of those rare specimens.

It all started when his folks used to take him and his brothers and sisters down to the Mozambique coast for their annual holidays. That was in the days before 1974 when Mozambique was still ruled by the experienced and civilised Portuguese and before the communist takeover which brought the country to a state of ruin and killed hundreds of thousands of people in the process.

Hamish loved being in the ocean which was kept warm by the Agulhas current that flows down the east African coast from the tropical areas of the Indian Ocean. He was a real sea baby and, by the age of nine, was riding a surfboard in the small to medium waves that broke on the beach where the family always stayed in rondavels (round native huts) right on the sand. Hamish learned the art of waveriding by watching a group of South African surfers who had driven their battered panel van all the way north in order to avoid the Christmas crowds on the beaches of Natal.

Another family who always stayed there at the same time were the Strydoms, a good, honest Boer clan who raised sheep and cattle on their ranch in the Northern Transvaal of South Africa.

While the two fathers sat on the beach, drinking Manica beer and discussing cattle prices, Hamish and his friend, Christian Strydom, used to get out in the surf and try to ride every wave that came their way. In the process they built up a solid friendship that was based on a common love of the surf. They hooted each other when they scored particularly good rides and gave advice to each other on how to improve; both of them were imaginative and liked to experiment.

However, all this came to an end in 1974 when the Portuguese were driven out of Mozambique and it reverted to a state of savagery. By then twenty year old Christian was studying at an agricultural college near Pretoria and Hamish, a corporal in the Rhodesian Light Infantry, was constantly on patrol trying to protect outlying farms in eastern Rhodesia from attacks by Mugabe's murdering terrorists. He enjoyed being out in the open but missed the waves terribly. When his much earned leave came due it coincided with the holidays at Christian's agricultural college and so the two chums decided to go on a two week surfing trip.

The moment he took leave of the Army at Old Cranbourne Barracks in Salisbury Hamish jumped into his Landrover and drove south to the Strydom farm near Pietersburg in the Northern Transvaal where he was received with the usual kind hospitality for which the Boers are justly famous.

He and Christian talked late into the night, poring over road maps as they tried to decide where to go. It was summer and they knew that all the beaches in Natal and the Cape would be crowded. Since neither of them would get the chance to surf again for another year they did not particularly want to spend any of their precious time fighting for waves in a crowded line-up and so they decided to go to some place where they would have the ocean to themselves.

Since they were both in a fairly reckless mood after a fine meal and plenty of excellent Cape wine they decided to be really radical and drive all the way to the coast of southern Angola, on the west coast of Central Africa, which was rumoured to have wonderful, uncrowded waves.

Angola was another Portuguese colony that was experiencing turmoil as a result of the communist coup in Lisbon but the fighting was mainly in the north and the interior and, as Christian remarked, it might well be the last opportunity to go there for some time. And anyway Hamish had taken the precaution of putting an Uzi sub-machine gun into the Landrover before leaving Salisbury.

After a hearty breakfast they set off early the next morning on their 1,500 mile journey, their boards, tents and cooking utensils in the back of the vehicle as well as a large hamper full of food that had been prepared by the thoughtful Mrs. Strydom.

They drove east and crossed the great Limpopo River into Botswana. Then across the empty veld to Francistown and over the hot, dry, rust red Kalahari desert to the tiny settlement of Ghanzi where they stopped for dinner at the only roadhouse.

They took it in turns to drive through the night across the desert and reached the town of Windhoek in South-West Africa just as the sun was rising. They decided to stop at a hotel for breakfast and a few hours kip so as to avoid the worst of the day's heat. In mid afternoon they set off on the final leg of their epic journey - through the emptiness of Damaraland and Ovamboland and into Angola.

The dawn was just breaking as the Landrover, covered in dust and grime, reached the top of a green hill. Below them lay a crescent shaped bay with a reef running out from a rocky point. Breaking over it were the most perfectly formed waves that either of them had ever seen.

Hamish put the vehicle into low gear and negotiated the steep, winding road down to the coast. The further they went, the worse the road became. When they finally pulled up at a spot where the deeply rutted and pot-holed track touched the sand they got out to inspect their surroundings.

To the south were bush clad hills that came right down to the sea but the land to the north had been cleared and they could see a plantation of sugar and banana trees. On a small rise in the middle of this productive unit stood a big, white plantation house with a wide verandah around it. Scattered here and there were a few native huts made of wattle and daub but that was all. At this early hour the only movement was a couple of baboons in the tree above them.

Although they were utterly exhausted after their long drive through four countries they couldn't resist going in for a quick surf - to feel the pleasure of immersing themselves in the ocean and to experience the thrill of riding a wave again after so many months out of the water.

They put on their board shorts, waxed their sticks and ran all the way down the beach as happy as larks. "Yuk!" cried Hamish. "This water is bloody cold." No longer the warm, fast flowing Agulhas current of the Indian Ocean but the freezing Benguela current that is born in the ice of the Antarctic and rolls up the southern ocean, hitting Africa at the Cape of Good Hope and then flowing all the way up the west coast to southern Angola. But the cold water did not dampen their ardour for their favourite element.

Later that afternoon, as they were dozing under a palm tree at the top of the beach, they were roused by the "clip-clop" sound of a horse which was approaching from the direction of the plantation house.

They sat up and saw a Portuguese man with a big, black moustache and a wide-brimmed panama hat who was riding towards them. When he caught their eye he took off his hat and waved it in the air by way of greeting.

He dismounted from his horse and they stood up and introduced themselves with much shaking of hands. It was Senhor Pereira whose family had built up the plantation over the course of three generations. He invited them to stay at the big house on the grounds that, because of the unstable political situation, visitors were few and far between and any company was more than welcome. They politely declined, explaining that they had come to surf and would prefer to put up their tents on the grass above the beach where they would be close to the waves and would not disturb anyone. However, they did accept his invitation to dinner that evening and he rode off to tell his wife that there would be two extra mouths at the table.

Senhor Pereira was thirty-five and his pretty, dark haired wife was a few years younger. They had two children, a boy, Joao, who was ten, and little Maria who was eight. Both Hamish and Christian could speak the rudiments of Portuguese which they had picked up during their many annual trips to Mozambique.

As they feasted on the fresh seafood both Senhor Pereira and his wife asked the boys many questions about surfing, about why they decided to come all the way to this neck of the woods to ride the waves and, of course, about the deteriorating security situation in southern Africa which was threatening the stability of all their countries - Rhodesia, Angola and ultimately South Africa.

Little Joao listened to all the surf talk with keen ears and asked if he could go out with them the next day on one of their surfboards. "No," said his father. "You can not swim and no one should ever go in the sea if they can't swim."

After dinner Senhora Pereira went off to put the children to bed and the three men sat on the wide verandah, with its low, overhanging thatch roof, drinking Mateus Rosé and talking of many things.

The two visitors could see that Senhor Pereira was depressed, which was not surprising as half of Angola was in a state of civil war and anarchy and it would only be a matter of time before this peaceful and beautiful part of the country would be caught up in the flames. "I will have to go to Portugal," he said sadly, "even though I have never been there in my life. And neither has my wife. We are third generation here. We will leave with nothing as the black men who are now in power - communists - are searching all the Portuguese as they get on the ships and are taking everything off them - even gold wedding rings and watches. Oh, what a terrible world it is! These blacks are not nearly ready to govern themselves but that is something that the stupid Western governments refuse to understand. The British and the Americans keep pushing for the blacks to have control but they won't be around to pick up the pieces when it all goes wrong."

"Listen, I have to spend several months a year out in the bush fighting the terrorists and this is my annual leave," said Hamish. "I'm trying to forget about all the chaos around us. Problem is that Africa is so bloody beautiful and awesome - like here - but it's also very screwed up."

He looked out at the dark ocean that was twinkling with a million lights from the stars above. And the crash of the breaking waves promised some good surf on the morrow. He wondered at the amazing world that had been created for Man and at the terrible way that Man has abused it with pollution, bloody wars and, the most evil thing of all, politics - which brings out the lowest instincts in men and which has caused more human misery than all the floods, earthquakes, fires and droughts put together.

The next day was hot and balmy and the two surfers spent many hours riding the waves that rolled into the bay. In the evening the Pereira family came down to the beach on their evening walk and Joao once again nagged his father to be allowed to go in the sea. Senhor Pereira repeated his refusal but did say that, once the boy had learned how to swim, he would be allowed to go on a surfboard. However, that would be difficult as neither Senhor Pereira nor his wife knew how to swim and there would be no one to teach him.

Certainly nothing had been done by the last evening of the surfers' stay when they were both out in the waves, trying to get the most out of the final few hours of their holiday. The waves were bigger than ever and not quite so clean but that only made the challenge all the greater.

Since it was their last day the Pereiras wanted to get some photos of them and so they brought their cameras down and stood on the rocky point to take some shots of Christian and Hamish as they powered across the faces of some very big waves. Knowing that they were being captured on film they tried some real show-off manoeuvres that didn't always succeed.

Joao had his own camera and he stepped down on to a lower ledge of rock in order to get a better shot of Hamish who was about to take off on a really huge mountain of water that was rolling in from outside. The wave broke and threw itself over the reef. Hamish was up and riding it and Joao took another photo. Suddenly the wave hit the rock with great force and swept the little boy into the foaming sea.

Then came the backwash that sucked him out into the Atlantic. The other Pereiras had run to the top of the rocks to avoid the big wave and it was a few seconds before they realised that Joao was not with them.

From his vantage point on the wave Hamish could see what had happened so he called out to Christian and they paddled as fast as they could to where the boy was madly swinging his arms and legs in a desperate effort to stay afloat.

Christian got there first and put his big, strong arm around Joao's shaking body. He uttered soothing words as he tried to keep the boy's head out of the water. But he had swallowed some sea water and it was necessary to get him on land in order to give mouth-to-mouth resuscitation.

By now Hamish had arrived on the scene but they were still several yards out from the rocks. Fortunately there was a lull in the sets so they put him on Christian's surfboard and pushed him to the nearest rocky point as fast as they could. Then they lifted him up on to a ledge that was well above the water line and took turns at kneeling down on the sharp rocks and giving him the kiss of life.

The rest of the Pereiras were also kneeling down on the rocks, frantically making the sign of the cross and praying to the Virgin Mary to bring their son back to life.

Their efforts and prayers were rewarded a few seconds later when colour started to come back into Joao's cheeks and he opened his eyes. A few minutes later he smiled and asked where his camera was. Somewhere in the Atlantic.

It was a silent and chastened family who returned to the house and somehow the political problems that faced them took on a lesser significance. They had literally lost their beloved only son and then he was restored to them - thanks to the efforts of Christian and Hamish. "Ah yes," thought Senhor Pereira, "those two boys must be rewarded. After all, if it was not for them Joao would not be with us to-night."

When Hamish and Christian called at the Pereira house shortly after dark to say good-bye (they were leaving first thing the next morning) they were led on to the verandah by their host and were told to sit down in the cane chairs while the cook brewed some coffee.

"Coffee and cakes to-night," said Senhor Pereira. "Not good to drink too much Mateus when you have to drive all that way to-morrow."

The coffee was served as well as two small banana cakes which were not much bigger than muffins. Senhor Pereira passed the cakes to the boys and they took one each.

"What are they?" asked Hamish politely.

"Banana cakes. From the bananas on our plantation. Very special cakes. They are soft but you must chew them gently as sometimes they are hard on the inside. Be careful, I don't want you to break your teeth."

The two surfers did as they were told but it wasn't long before each of them came into contact with a very hard object. Far too hard to bite and certainly too big to swallow. What sort of trick was this?

Almost simultaneously they took the things out of their mouths and stared at them. They were still coated with chewed cake so Hamish picked up some tissues from the table and began to wipe his one clean. Christian did the same. As the chewed muck was wiped away they found themselves staring at two of the largest diamonds they had ever seen. Each was as big as a thumbnail (and the top of the thumb as well). Large and beautiful enough to be in the Crown Jewels.

"What is this?" asked a surprised Christian.

"My way of saying thank-you for saving my son's life this afternoon."

"But what we did was quite normal. Any surfer would have done it. It wasn't as if we were risking our lives. We surf in that type of sea all the time."

"Maybe, but I couldn't do anything because I can not swim," he replied. "What you did meant the difference between life and death. So this is my way of thanking you."

"But in South Africa, when someone is rescued by the lifesavers, they hardly say thank-you. Often they don't even send a donation to the surf lifesaving club," said Christian.

"I am not in South Africa and this is what I want to do."

"I didn't realise that there were such big diamonds in Angola," said an amazed Hamish.

"Oh yes," said Senhor Pereira with a knowing smile. "The Oppenheimers don't get their greedy hands on all of Africa's diamonds."

With effusive thanks (the two surfers for the diamonds and the Pereiras for saving the life of their son) Hamish and Christian said their good-byes and then walked back to their tents. As soon as they were out of earshot Hamish said, "Well, that is certainly the best cake I've ever tasted."

"Yes," replied Christian, "and next year we can go anywhere we like for our surfing holiday. What about Hawaii?"

CHAPTER SIXTEEN

SPIRIT OF SURFING

Friday, 13th September, 1997, was not a good day for Barney Brentford. He spent the morning in his office at the surf clothing company where he worked in Southern California. It was a busy day as he had to prepare for his coming business trip to Europe as well as study the latest sales figures. They were not good and he, as sales manager, would be the one to take the rap. These days he always seemed to be taking the rap for one thing or another. It would not be so bad if the manager, Bill Nolan, was not such a temperamental bastard but he was and Barney and the rest of the staff just had to put up with it.

Barney was forty-nine last birthday and had been working in the same company for fifteen years. He had originally been taken on because he had made a name for himself in surfing by winning the so-called world championship back in the 1960s when the prize for such a feat was a cup worth twenty-five pounds. These days the World Champion could earn a million dollars a year. Barney sometimes wondered if he had been born at the wrong time but, when he really thought about it, he decided that that was not the case.

He might be underpaid and doing a job that he found more and more boring but that was a small price to pay for the supreme pleasure of living, surfing and growing to manhood in those wonderful years of the Sixties when every day seemed to be a whole new world filled with infinite possibilities. A time when he and the other surfers were exploring new horizons and enjoying the magical experience of being the first ones to ride some of the world's best waves that were currently being discovered in new and exotic locations. An age when the spirit of surfing meant that you shared your thrills and adventures with all the others of the small tribe in a spirit of human communion not felt before or since.

It seemed like the dawn of a new age when all the conventions and restrictions that had suffocated man since time immemorial were being stripped away. When a sad, grey world was suddenly splashed with colour. Wonderful music, weird dreams and amazing clothes. When anything seemed possible. Oh yes, Barney might be impoverished by the standards of some of to-day's highly paid pro surfers but he would not swap places with them for anything. Especially the current World Champion whom he had seen surfing down at the local beach the previous week-end.

It had been more like a circus than a surf session. Why, just to get into the water the poor chap had to fight his way through more than a hundred screaming groupies who were struggling to touch him. And then some of the heavy locals kept dropping in on him just to let him know that, although he might be World Champion, this was their beach. And how could you enjoy a surf when there were two helicopters buzzing only a few feet above you just to get some hot photos for the next issue of the magazines? How could anyone surf with all that noise and distraction? "Surfing is meant to be a pleasure - not a bloody ordeal," thought Barney. "The true spirit of surfing seems to be well and truly dead."

At lunchtime he drove down to the beach in his old Chevvy for a midday surf. The waves were really crowded and, as he looked along to both his left and his right, he could see one long line-up of surfers that seemed to stretch from the Mexican border all the way to Rincon. He could remember surfing the same beach as a kid and being the only one out.

He went for a wave but someone dropped in on him. He tried again but the same thing happened. He thought again about the lost spirit of surfing. He then caught a big one and sped across its face. A nicely formed barrel opened in front of him and he ducked low into it. Things were looking up. He paddled back to the line-up in the hope of finding some space on another one.

To his right an argument was taking place between a young shortboarder with a shaven skull and an older longboarder who looked like an ex-Marine. Some loud and vicious words were being exchanged, with the longboarder being accused of dropping in and taking up too much space in the water with his "bloody great aircraft carrier".

"Piss off, punk," called the craggy faced mal rider.

Other longboarders paddled over and so did some of the "punk's" friends and it quickly became a free-for-all. Another mal rider punched the cheeky young punk in the face and was immediately attacked from behind by one of the victim's mates.

Barney looked at his waterproof watch and saw that it was time to go in so he waited for an incoming set and took the third wave. Miraculously no one dropped in and he scored a magic ride.

On the beach he put on his business shirt and fawn walk shorts and then went up to the kiosk to have a blueberry muffin and a cup of coffee.

The sound of raised voices caused him to look down the beach. Three of the shortboarders were running along with their boards under their arms. They were being chased by some of the longboarders who were screaming abuse and splashing them with water. The argument that started out in the line-up had now washed up on the beach and more punches were being thrown.

Barney saw one of the shortboarders run up the beach to a van. A minute later he was running along the sand with a Smith and Wesson .38 calibre revolver in his hand.

The next minute a shot ran out. Then another. One of the longboarders fell down in the shallow water. Blood was starting to flow out of his chest and a little puddle of purple was appearing in the otherwise turquoise sea.

People were running in all directions - including the gunman who was sprinting back to his van. But he did not get there.

A cop who was on the promenade saw what had happened. He drew his police pistol and pointed it at the running figure. He opened fire and the shortboarder fell to the ground. Dead.

There were now two corpses on the beach and Barney just wanted to get away from it all. Even his boring old office now seemed an attractive place of refuge. "That's it," he thought as he unlocked the door of the Chevvy. "Battles in the line-up, blood in the sea, blood on the beach; it's like a war zone. The old spirit of surfing is now as dead as the dodo."

By now police sirens could be heard all over the place as carloads of heavily armed cops zoomed in from all directions, some of them excited at the prospect of maybe shooting some surfers. Barney could even see a helicopter gunship arriving through the smog from the east. It reminded him of Vietnam.

Back in the office he suffered a further blow. His manager came in and told him that, instead of spending all of the next week in south-west France as he had hoped, the programme had been changed. He would now be at the trade show in Biarritz for only three days and would then have to go on to Scotland to present the prizes - and, of course, promote the company's products - at the Western Highlands surf club.

This really was the last straw. He had been looking forward to getting his business done in Biarritz and then staying on to surf the wonderful waves of the Basque country. And now that was being taken away from him and he was being sent to Scotland instead. It was a place he had never been to or had any desire to visit.

"And what is it about this Western Highlands surf club that makes it so important?" he asked his manager.

"I know the club president, Malcolm McMurdoch."

"So?"

"I met him twenty years ago in Bali. He did me a favour."

"What? Did he buy you a drink?"

"No. The night before I was leaving I got into a spot of bother with the police over a bag of Sumatran buds. Anyway, the cops threatened to put me in gaol for seven years if I didn't come up with sufficient bribe money. I tried to explain that it was my last night and I had only ten bucks left but they insisted on a hundred dollars and not a cent less. I managed to persuade them to take me to the Three Monkeys bar where I hoped to see someone I knew who might be able to help me out. Unfortunately, none of my buddies were there but this chap McMurdoch was having a drink on his own.

I had once said 'good-day' to him in the line-up and, being desperate, told him of my predicament. Without batting an eyelid he reached into his pocket and pulled out a hundred dollar note and handed it to the police. I was a free man again. Of course, I sent him the money as soon as I got back here and we've sent each other Christmas cards ever since.

He has helped form this surf club in Scotland and they're having their first club competition. He wants to have some big name from the present or the past to hand out the prizes. It's the first time he's ever asked me for a favour and, in view of the fact that he kept me out of gaol for seven years, I really can't turn him down. Besides, it will be a good chance to do some P.R. for the company. Make sure you take plenty of boardshorts along."

"I'd say wetsuits and booties would be more appropriate for that part of the world," replied a dejected Barney.

"Good on you; I knew you wouldn't let me down," said the manager as he strode out of the office.

Barney cleared his desk, packed his briefcase and then went downstairs to collect some samples and stock to take to Europe. But, try as he might, he could not get the image of the carnage on the beach out of his mind. Nor could he help comparing what he had seen with the peace and good feeling that he had known all those years ago when the waves were a place of pleasure and friendship - not death.

It rained the whole time in Biarritz and the sea was rough and unrideable. However, he did manage to negotiate some satisfactory new business for his company which, he mused, should keep the manager from blowing his top for a while. And so to Scotland.

He arrived at Glasgow Airport just before midday and hired a car for the journey north. "I suppose I'll just have to make the most of it," he thought. "Thank God I'm here for only two days."

He began to wonder if perhaps he should not have spent quite so much of his youth chasing waves. If only he had taken up a trade he would now be a self-employed plumber or electrician earning good money and choosing his jobs instead of being sent to God forsaken places in order to repay twenty year old favours for his temperamental manager who, he reflected, should never have been so stupid as to get into the situation with the Indonesian police in the first place.

However, his mood began to change as he drove up the western side of the silent and beautiful Loch Lomond. It reminded him of the old folk song that he had learned at school. He had been to many places in the world to surf but he never dreamed that he would one day be making his way along the "bonnie, bonnie banks o' Loch Lomon' ".

He drove on through the green wooded hills of Glencoe and stopped at a Scotch whisky distillery for a wee taste of the company's product.

Then on past towns with romantic names like Fort William and Fort Augustus until he reached Loch Ness. The Monster was nowhere to be seen - only a solitary kilted figure standing at the water's edge playing a mournful dirge on the bagpipes. Barney was fast being won over by the awesome beauty of the wild and lonely Highlands. They seemed to be almost untouched by the modern world and they reminded him of what the plains and Rockies of North America must have been like in the days of the Indian.

He turned off at Inverness and eventually reached his destination on the lonely north coast of Scotland in the early evening. As he was driving over the last spur the ocean suddenly came into view; all he could see were long lines of perfectly formed waves breaking over a reef that stretched out from a rocky point on which stood a crumbling castle. There were half a dozen black wetsuit clad figures on their sticks - both short boards and mals - who were taking wave after wave after wave.

Barney pulled up at the top of the beach and got out of his car to the cry of the seagulls and the smell of kelp. He took his board out of the back of the hatchback, put on a wetsuit and ran into the sea. It was not nearly as cold as he expected as the North Atlantic current, flowing on from the Gulf stream, warms these far northern seas.

When he reached the line-up the other surfers all paddled over to him, introduced themselves and shook hands. Every one of them thanked him for coming and said how stoked they were to have such a famous name come all the way from California to surf "our wee break".

A powerful set was rolling in. "Go on, Barney, your wave," they shouted as the ex-world champion felt the mounting rush of water under his board. He paddled fast and jumped up just in time to see a round, hollow barrel forming in front of him.

In he went and for a few wonderful seconds he experienced that magical feeling he had felt so often before but which seemed to be a new thrill every time - being totally encompassed in the ocean's womb. No other existence except you and the wave.

It was the first surf he'd had since leaving Los Angeles and, when he came out of the tube and emerged through the white water, it was to the sound not of gunfire but of hooting and cheering from the locals.

"Gee, that's one of the best rides we've ever seen; we're so glad you've come. We hope to learn a few tricks from you. Go on, take another wave; we want to watch." He did; it was not quite as good as the first but he enjoyed it all the same.

Those words: "Go on, take another wave." He had not heard anything like that for a long time. It was usually something like "Get out of my way, you silly old fart." And they said they were stoked at having a "name" surfer (even from another era). Why, it was only last month that the World

Champion had gone to surf the Rivermouth at Ventura in California and the jealous little locals had let down all the tyres of his car.

"Where is Malcolm McMurdoch?" asked Barney when they were back on the beach. "He's the chap I'm meant to be staying with to-night."

"He's not surfing to-day; he went shooting instead. He should be home by now. He knew you were coming and wanted to give you some fresh venison. We'll drive you to his house."

Malcolm was about forty-five and had the weathered and dour face of a Highland farmer but his eyes lit up when he met Barney. He kept saying how privileged they were to have him in their little neck of the woods - even though it was for only a couple of nights. "I met your boss in Bali many years ago," he said.

"Yes, so he told me," replied Barney.

It seemed that the entire local surfing crew turned up at Malcolm's farmhouse that night for a supper that consisted of a haunch of venison served with chestnuts and prunes. Longboarders and shortboarders, farmers in tweed jackets, fishermen in dungarees and tartan bush jackets and students in black leather pants and garish shirts - all were united in their love of surfing and their desire to see the ocean rid of pollution.

"So you don't have a crowd problem here?" remarked Barney wryly.

"Not at all. Our club has got only a couple of dozen members and it's not often that everyone is in the water at the same time."

"Do you ever have any out-of-town surfers pass through?"

"Occasionally. We really like to surf with others and get to know them. Last month a couple of American surfers came. They stayed for a week. We were sorry to see them leave."

"Well, just make sure they don't feature your break in a surf magazine. You might not be happy with the result," said Barney.

The next morning he surfed with them again and in the evening there was a booze up at the surf club which, Barney was surprised to discover, was situated inside the old grey castle that stood on the rocky point.

"It hadn't been used for more than four hundred years," explained Malcolm. "It was a strongpoint during the clan wars. Anyway, we fitted it out with a wee bar and the laddies hang their wetsuits to dry over the turret. There's a narrow stone staircase that leads up to the top of the tower where they used to look out for the enemy but we only ever go up there to do a surf check."

Barney duly did the honours and presented the prizes. He then gave a short speech about his company, its products and surfing in general. Then Malcolm announced that they were going to show a surf video. He apologised to Barney for showing such an old one but it was the only one they had.

"Which one is it?" asked Barney.

"Morning of the Earth."

"But that's my favourite!" exclaimed the visitor. "One of the first surf movies ever made; it shows surfing in its purest and most beautiful form."

"Then it should bring back some memories for you," replied Malcolm as he turned on the video.

On his first day back at work Barney went into the manager's office to report on his trip. After he had outlined the deals that he had made at the trade show the manager looked up and said, "Anything else?"

"Yes."

"What?"

"I rediscovered something."

"What's that?"

"The true spirit of surfing

CHAPTER SEVENTEEN

SURFERS' RIGHTS

In my last book of surfing stories, *Deep Inside*, I ended with a chapter on the pollution of the sea as this is a threat to every surfer. Unfortunately, it is not the only threat and I am going to end the present volume with a chapter on the growing threat to surfers' rights that is posed by the authorities.

Ever since surfing began we have always taken it for granted that, whenever we see a clean and powerful wave breaking over a reef or point, we can grab our boards and paddle out to enjoy it. Sounds pretty regular, doesn't it? Unfortunately, such a scenario is increasingly under threat by the law which these days can not refrain from keeping its interfering nose out of any human activity.

Surfing is a sport for individuals - just the man and the wave. Sadly, in the twenty - first century, the individual has become an endangered species. We are to-day living under the tyranny of law as the bossy types who goven us do not trust us to do anything on our own initiative and so they have drowned us in a sea of restrictions, bans and petty little laws and regulations.

What they especially hate is to see young people enjoying themselves - which is why we have the oppressive and entirely ineffective drug laws, the permanent police blitz against young drivers, the increasing restrictions for buying, advertising and smoking cigarettes, the anti-noise laws which empower men in uniform to barge into private houses and rip the stereo out of its socket and, the most sinister of all, the Criminal Justice Act 1994 which was introduced by Michael Howard, the Home Secretary in the last Conservative Government. This nasty little law prohibits a person from having a party on his own property if:

a) there are more than a hundred guests
b) it is held outdoors, and
c) techno music is played (even at low volume)

If these three conditions are present, a cop can enter on to the private property where the party is being held and arrest the host without warrant *even if there has not been any complaint from the neighbours*. Section 65 of this evil law states that, if a cop "reasonably believes" that a person is on his way to such a party, he (the policeman) can stop him and prevent him proceeding anywhere within five miles of the site of the party. And how do the cops exercise this "reasonable belief"? By using section 65 against any person under the age of twenty-five who comes into their line of sight.

If the partygoer (or any other young person who is grabbed under this section) should value the traditional right of the citizen to freedom of movement and thereby refuses to comply with the request, he can be arrested on the spot without a warrant and can be convicted and fined. So, thanks to the Criminal Justice Act, it can now be a crime to walk along the street in a peaceful manner just as it was in Nazi Germany and Soviet Russia.

One of the pleasures of beach life on a warm summer's evening is having a barbecue on the sand but even that little pleasure is denied to us by the wretched councils. It constitutes a "trespass" and the authorities spend a lot of money to prevent such a terrible crime from taking place - including police helicopters flying up and down the coast in summer looking for parties around a campfire and then sending a message to the cops on the ground to go all the way to some remote part of the beach in the middle of the night to bust up a happy party. And this in a country like Britain where there are more than a million burglaries a year that the police don't even try to solve!

Bans are now the order of the day. If there is some activity that the know-alls in government decide is not good for our health or safety or anything else, then they slap a ban on it. What they are really doing is showing their contempt for each and every one of us and for democracy itself because the essence of democracy is that many different types of people live together and pursue their various interests, while having tolerance for the activities of others.
Unfortunately, the new intolerance of individual rights can not even leave us alone in the water.

The source of the problem - and many others - lies in the American mania for suing people. If you accidentally tread on someone's toe on a busy New York pavement, you can be sued for millions of dollars and have your whole life ruined.

Similarly, if a surfer in the waves accidentally injures a swimmer, then the swimmer can sue the local council which is allegedly responsible for ensuring everyone's safety at the beach. There are even lawyers with not much work to do who cruise up and down the beaches in Los Angeles looking for such a situation *or even creating it.*

The idea is that you don't sue the surfer whose board hit you because he probably doesn't have any money. Instead, you sue the local council for not providing beaches that are safe for swimmers and they will have to pay out millions of dollars to the injured man which they then have to get back by increasing the rates that the property owners must pay. When the rates go up, the ratepayers bring pressure on the council to remove the threat of further huge claims for similar types of accidents and the easiest way to do that is to ban surfing from all the beaches in the council area.

Such a nightmare scenario actually occurred in Hong Kong early in 1997 when it was still under British rule. A swimmer complained to the Hong Kong Urban Council of being hit by a surfboard and so the Council, fearful of a similar thing happening again in which case they might be sued, put up signs which banned surfing and required surfers to apply for a permit up to two months in advance *each time* they would want to go into the waves with their surfboard. Anyone who broke this ridiculous law had to pay a fine of Hong Kong $2,000 (about £160). So, a couple of surfs without permission would cost you as much as a new surfboard! The ban was enforced by lifeguards with the back-up of police.

This raises another point: the beach should be a place of freedom where people can relax and lie in the sun and listen to music and do what they like so long as they don't harm others. However, councils are bringing in more and more by-laws to restrict what you can do on the sand. For example, at Santa Monica beach in Los Angeles there is a huge sign at the entrance to the beach that takes several minutes to read. It lists all the things that people are not allowed to do on the sand. There are hefty fines for playing music on the beach, for putting up a tent or canvas windbreak, for walking your dog, changing your clothes or even going to sleep in the sun.

One of the worst aspects of all these restrictions is that it brings on to the beach a whole lot of unwanted law enforcers. At Santa Monica gun wielding cops patrol the sand, watch everybody like spies and never hesitate to pull people up for the tiniest infraction of the stupid regulations. Meanwhile, a few blocks inland, the streets are controlled by gun totin' gangs of violent criminals; the police never venture anywhere near these no-go areas. They are too busy targeting those dangerous members of the public who go to the beach and might fall asleep or play a guitar on the sand. Such are the twisted priorities of the rather cowardly Los Angeles Police Department. And anyway, who wants to see cops on the beach? Most sane people would rather eye the bikini beauties than a bunch of fat, ugly policewomen.

On the surfing beaches of France one also has to put up with the heavy hand of authority. Although they don't mind you playing music or going to sleep or even taking off all your clothes, there is still a nasty vibe in the water in August when the uniformed thugs of the C.R.S. (France's riot police) are given a soft transfer for a month; instead of whacking their batons on people's heads during Paris demonstrations (which they do for eleven months of the year) the Government sends them to the surf beaches of south-west France to "assist" the lifeguards to enforce "regulations" as to which part of the sea you can surf in and which part you can't.

These overweight, crew-cutted apes prowl up and down the beach in their badly fitting T-shirts with "C.R.S." emblazoned all over them looking for trouble. If you are a head basher for eleven months of the year, facing unruly demonstrators, then it must be quite hard to be "nice" for the other month.

Their most favoured tactic is to stand at the water's edge and bawl out to some surfer whose magic ride might have taken him a foot or two over an imaginary line in the sea that is supposed to separate the swimmers from the surfers. If you don't come in immediately, then either the lifeguard or the ape will paddle out and physically grab you and the board. Their usual trick is to confiscate the board for a few days or even a week and make you pay a hefty fine to get it back again. Gone are the days when the lifeguard's job was to save lives; these days some of them are so busy throwing their weight around that they wouldn't have time to notice if someone was drowning.

One of the most cunning ways that governments "justify" their ban on things is the four letter word "cost". That's the stated reason behind the smoking ban; smokers can get sick and cost the health service money for their treatment and so smoking has to be restricted by law. "Cost" is also the reason for the compulsory wearing of "safety" helmets on motor bikes and now, in Australia and New Zealand, on push bikes as well. And sooner or later they will use the same spurious argument to require every surfer to wear an expensive "protective" helmet in the water. All it needs is for one surfer to suffer a severe head injury and for it to get on the front page of the tabloids and then the whole legislative apparatus of London and Brussels will spring into action with a plethora of new laws and regulations of a restrictive nature.

Over-reaction to single and isolated instances is the new order of the day and to hell with anyone's rights.

One little girl gets savaged by a pit-bull terrier and, bingo, the Government introduces the Dangerous Dogs Act which prohibits anyone in the United Kingdom from owning a pit bull terrier. (Penalty: six months imprisonment plus a fine).

One lunatic with a gun commits a terrible massacre at Dunblane and, bingo, every farmer, hunter and other person in the British Isles had to give up their hand guns. (But the I.R.A terrorists were allowed to keep their guns. And why not? After all they are so responsible with guns, aren't they?)

One stampede occurs at a football match and, bingo, every sports ground in Britain has to be "upgraded" to a "higher safety standard" at a cost of hundreds of millions of pounds. Even Wimbledon, where they have never had a stampede in 125 years and never would, had to fork out millions of pounds to comply with the new "safety requirements" instead of applying its money to more worthwhile purposes like tennis coaching in schools.

And one serious head injury to a surfer that is featured in the tabloids and, bingo, every one of us will be forced by law to wear an expensive helmet and will be fined if we don't. This will bring more cops and other law enforcers on to the beach and surfing will be that much less free and enjoyable than it is at present.

If you become a competitive surfer and enter contests the government will take an even closer and more sinister interest in you; they'll even go to the unbelievable length of inspecting your urine!

The current tabloid fuelled mania about drugs in sport means that every sports body (including the British Surfing Association) that accepts money from the government's Sports Council must, as a condition of receiving a grant, extend a warm hand of welcome to people from the "Doping Control Unit" who by law have the right to turn up at any contest and require any competitor to piss into a bottle!

Since surfing, unlike athletics and cycling, is not a sport where performance enhancing drugs like steroids would be of any benefit, the only purpose of such tests on surfers is law enforcement. In other words, to have a nosey peek at what the surfer might have smoked, drunk or taken in the past few days. Urine tests should have no place in surfing because they are unnecessary. It is no way to treat a surfer or indeed any human being. Only animals - like racehorses - should have urine taken from them by force.

Urine tests are all part of the "war against drugs" which is less about suppressing drugs than providing the government with an excuse to breach people's rights and violate their bodies in a way that would otherwise not be acceptable.

One can only imagine what types of people would be attracted to a job in the "Doping Control Unit". Job satisfaction is a big factor in most people's employment and no doubt the prospect of playing around with bottles of other people's warm urine has its attractions for some.

The yellow liquid is then taken away and God knows what happens to it. The weird characters who have chosen to make their careers in the "Doping Control Unit" claim that they "analyse" it but who knows what they really do with it? When it gets down to that level, anything is possible. Of course it is sick and disgusting and is the type of thing that one would have expected from the perverted doctors and control freaks of the Third Reich. *But it is the law! In Britain! To-day!*

So long as the British Surfing Association continues to accept the grotty money from the Sports Council in return for subjecting surfers to the unnecessary and degrading treatment of urine tests, it is hardly surprising that so many of Britain's top surfers stay away from contests. They should be commended for upholding their human dignity and the freedom to surf without letting the authorities interfere with their most private parts.

And that's not all. If a surfer flies back to Britain from a place like Bali to surf in a contest he could well have several of his private orifices "inspected" by the authorities.

If the customs officer at the airport is jealous of a young surfer being able to afford a surf trip to exotic places, he can satisfy his envy, not to mention any queer tendencies, by what is euphemistically called an "intimate body search". In other words, an act of rape by the State. Of course, it is all done in the name of the "war against drugs" - a war which the government lost years ago but has never had the courage or honesty to admit it. Anyway, if they didn't use this as their excuse to put their finger up the citizen's bum, they would soon think of something else. Diamonds perhaps.

After this first violation of his body our notional surfer gets into a car to drive to the contest. On the road he can be pulled up by a cop for any reason or for no reason and have another orifice violated by having to provide some of his breath into a plastic bag. And then, when he finally reaches the contest, he can be attacked by the kinky urine brigade.

And it's getting worse! In 1998 police in Lancashire, Strathclyde, Sussex and Cleveland started testing thousands of drivers with hand held "drug testers" which require the driver to contribute either his saliva or the sweat on his forehead to see if he might have committed the unpardonable crime of smoking a joint some time in the previous few weeks. Even if he had, it would not affect his driving. Although only in its initial stages, this gross infringement of personal privacy will soon become standard practice on roads throughout Britain. So, in addition to taking our breath and our urine and sticking fingers up people's bums, the authorities now want our sweat and our spit as well. That only leaves nose pickings and it will only be a matter of time before they find some reason to get their sordid hands on them as well. It's scary stuff. Besides being unnecessary and insulting to the individual, this pre-occupation of the government with our bodies is ever so vulgar. The individual should be the sole owner of his body and it should be off-limits to government snoops. But it's not.

They didn't have any of these nasty laws a few years ago, when we were governed by sensible and decent men like Churchill, and there is no reason to have them to-day - except to satisfy the government's insatiable craving to poke its dirty nose into every little aspect of our lives and bodies.

The Labour Government in Britain is really down on sport and on people having a good time. That is why they have redirected lottery money that was allocated for sport to other purposes and have banned sports from receiving sponsorship from the tobacco companies.

These sour faced killjoys are even trying to ban some sports altogether, starting with fox hunting. Once they've got that one out of the way, they'll start looking for another sport to ban and surfing could well be on their list.

If hunting is cruel, so is fishing and, if this curious reasoning is followed, then why not ban surfing because the speed of the fin slicing through the water might upset the fish and other sea creatures?

The real reason behind the proposed ban on hunting is not concern for the fox as they claim. The Members of Parliament who pretend to be so concerned about the life of a fox are the same ones who have such a callous disregard for human life that they give their whole hearted support to abortion. No, the real reason is that they just can not bear to see people enjoying themselves. Huntsmen are perceived as jolly types who like the good things of life. So are surfers. Hence the danger.

All sportsmen and sportswomen are in this one together and, if we don't want legislative restrictions on our own sport, we must vigorously defend the right of any person to engage in any sport for the simple reason that, if the government succeeds in banning one sport, it will only whet their appetite to ban others. The Olympic sport of pistol shooting has already been banned in Britain and they are trying to ban fox hunting. Where will surfing be on this list?

When laws start intruding into areas where they don't belong - like in the waves - the most sensible response is to ignore them altogether but make sure you don't get caught. Any laws that limit our right to surf should be treated with the contempt they deserve. If we don't defy that sort of legislative tyranny, then we don't deserve to surf.